NISI SHAWL

Winner of the
Tiptree Award
City Artist Program Award (Seattle)
and Nominated for the
Nebula Award
World Fantasy Award
Gaylactic Spectrum Award
Sturgeon Memorial Award

"Shawl's keen sense of justice and her adamant
anticolonialism always ride just beneath the surface of
her stories. Never didactic, Shawl possesses the gift of
a true storyteller: the ability to let the warp and weft
of plot and character do her moral work for her."
—Brian Charles Clark, *Curled Up with a Good Book*

"A talented and distinctive voice."
—Daniel Haeusser, *The Skiffy and Fanty Show*

"Nisi Shawl tells stories as if she has just awakened from a vivid
and terrifying dream, and she's intent on relating its details."
—*Seattle Times*

"Nisi's wit, in both her conversation and her
fiction, ranges from friv⋯⋯⋯⋯
mordant; for me, it rep⋯⋯
of response to the i⋯⋯
—L. Tim⋯

Talk like a Man

plus

PM PRESS OUTSPOKEN AUTHORS SERIES

1. *The Left Left Behind*
   Terry Bisson

2. *The Lucky Strike*
   Kim Stanley Robinson

3. *The Underbelly*
   Gary Phillips

4. *Mammoths of the Great Plains*
   Eleanor Arnason

5. *Modem Times 2.0*
   Michael Moorcock

6. *The Wild Girls*
   Ursula K. Le Guin

7. *Surfing the Gnarl*
   Rudy Rucker

8. *The Great Big Beautiful Tomorrow*
   Cory Doctorow

9. *Report from Planet Midnight*
   Nalo Hopkinson

10. *The Human Front*
    Ken MacLeod

11. *New Taboos*
    John Shirley

12. *The Science of Herself*
    Karen Joy Fowler

13. *Raising Hell*
    Norman Spinrad

14. *Patty Hearst & The Twinkie Murders: A Tale of Two Trials*
    Paul Krassner

15. *My Life, My Body*
    Marge Piercy

PM PRESS OUTSPOKEN AUTHORS SERIES

16. *Gypsy*
Carter Scholz

17. *Miracles Ain't What They Used to Be*
Joe R. Lansdale

18. *Fire.*
Elizabeth Hand

19. *Totalitopia*
John Crowley

20. *The Atheist in the Attic*
Samuel R. Delany

21. *Thoreau's Microscope*
Michael Blumlein

22. *The Beatrix Gates*
Rachel Pollack

23. *A City Made of Words*
Paul Park

24 *Talk like a Man*
Nisi Shawl

25 *Big Girl*
Meg Elison

Talk like a Man

plus

Women of the Doll

plus

An Awfully Big Adventure

and much more

Nisi Shawl

PM PRESS | 2020

Editor's note:

The author of this volume prefers to go by "they/them" pronouns, so this is reflected in the "About the Author" and other portions of this volume, but quotations from reviews that use "she/her" to refer to Shawl have not been altered where they appear in this book and retain use of "she" and "her."

"Walk like a Man" was published in *Bahamut* no. 1, Summer 2015.

"Women of the Doll" was published in *GUD* no. 1, Autumn 2007.

"Something More" was published in *Something More and More*, edited by L. Timmel Duchamp, Aqueduct Press, May 2011 (in celebration of Shawl's Guest of Honor status at WisCon 35).

"An Awfully Big Adventure" was published in the anthology *An Alphabet of Embers*, edited by Rose Lemberg, Stone Bird Press, 2016.

"Ifa: Reverence, Science, and Social Technology" is based on a speech given at Duke University on January 29, 2010. A version was published in *Extrapolation* 57, no. 1–2 (Spring/Summer 2016), the publication of the Science Fiction Research Association.

Talk like a Man
Nisi Shawl © 2020
This edition © PM Press
Series Editor: Terry Bisson

ISBN: 978-1-62963-711-2
LCCN: 2019933021

Cover design by John Yates/www.stealworks.com
Author photograph by Brian Charles Clarke
Insides by Jonathan Rowland

CONTENTS

Walk like a Man 1

Women of the Doll 13

Something More 45

An Awfully Big Adventure 81

Ifa: Reverence, Science, and Social Technology 84

"The Fly in the Sugar Bowl" 95
Nisi Shawl interviewed by Terry Bisson

Bibliography 105

About the Author 113

To my magnificent nieces, Brittany Shinel Johnson and
Aaliyah Mari Hudson, who talk like whatever they want.

Walk like a Man

SHAHDAY TUGGED AND SMOOTHED her blonde ponytail and said to me, "I'm thinking of starting a girlpack." She said it out loud, because this was in Social Studies at Riverdale. She had to be there in her meat along with everyone else. The idea was to prevent us from forgetting something important if we never did anything but teleprez.

Of course I paid attention. This was Shahday Brooke, one of the toppest of the top; the units were impressed she went to Riverdale, and whatever they say, I think that's why they enrolled me in that particular replica. They can be smart. Back when people like us were called black they had to be.

Took me a long time into the season till I scored a seat next to Shahday, trading favors like braiding hair and making bracelets for kids in my way. Hard work, but I wound up in the genuine wood-and-metal desk to Shahday's immediate right.

Which might be the only reason she even said that to me, the only reason I got to join her girlpack, the only reason for all what happened.

\#

I have an I. Is this less? Was we more? In a body. The many of us did this to become one me. The me is to become bigger.

Instant clothing; to see, I must look. The us left behind will only make a mirror if I ask. In words. I do.

Reflecting in it to better realize. Face am I. And hands with reaching. Touching. The flesh. The fabric hot, fresh; scent of it filling the small room.

#

"Who's your girlpack gonna belong to?" That was the best question I could come up with in response to what Shahday told me. Obvious. Stupid. I looked away, around the replica's room, the five rows of desks and chairs with other kids in them, the whiteboard at the front, the teacher writing on it in smelly red ink. A diagram of nothing I could use.

Shahday didn't bother answering, just turned toward her friend Lundun and said something low I couldn't quite hear. They laughed. Then they looked at me to be sure I knew who they were laughing at.

"Something interesting?" said the teacher. I think her name was Mrs. Schroeder. No sig in the meat, of course. "Would you care to share it with the whole class?"

Lundun smiled politely. "Kiss it."

The teacher froze up like a DOS attack. She was in the meat, not on, same as everybody in the replica, because that's the whole point of Riverdale. But I swear she looked exactly like she'd glitched.

Her eyes freed up and she blinked. Next came her hands, curling under her throat as if they weren't sure whether or not to grab each other. Her mouth opened and she ordered all three of us into detention.

"Fine," said Shahday. So I wasn't going to argue, even though I hadn't done too much really wrong. I went to detention with her and Lundun when the bell rang instead of out of the building home.

#

Words are loud now—loud as remembering. How to look for the widest way; how to be the most big. We gave me a plan. No better than to follow it. Find the god. In the grove.

First open the door. Blinding brightness. Swift adjustment. Step out. Turn right.

#

Riverdale's detention is in its own separate room. Why, nobody's ever told me. It runs after the regular school session. No detention during Social Studies, Gym, or Makering; they could have used any of those rooms. I guess maybe they didn't because this other space was already there.

We had to walk down the building's hall to get to it. The hall is a long, narrow place with huge glass windows on either side, slanting down a little hill. I went slow. Gave me time to think.

Lundun reached the door before Shahday and opened it. I came in after them, while the lights were still turning on. No windows. Blank walls, bare tables, plastic chairs. Nothing and nobody else. Detention was supposed to be boring, even more boring than the rest of the replica. Punishment. The exact opposite of getting on.

#

How I move forward is to walk. Which is like falling. Giving in to gravity. Balance and let go. No fright belongs with this experience because it is a major subroutine and I am assigned enough processor. And priority without request. Previously determined I would need this.

#

Shahday and Lundun slammed down across from each other at the table furthest from the door. From me. I made believe that was hunky dory and concentrated on undoing the flap of my expensive purse while sitting at the same table, other end. Like I didn't notice what I was doing. Pulled out a bag of chuck and gulped a slug.

That got their attention.

"Want some?" I held out the bag so either of them could take it.

"Sure." Shahday grabbed its cord. "How'd you get this, anyway, Lia?" The first time she'd called me by my name.

"You know." I shrugged. "The usual."

"Yeah." She wasn't going to admit she had no idea. Which meant I was under no obligation to explain how I stole it.

Shahday passed Lundun the bag. "That's kinda good!" Lundun said after a tiny swallow. She helped herself to another, bigger.

Riverdale's minder came over the room's speakers. "Atmospheric ester levels red," the AI announced. "Combined with camera data, we're forced to conclude you're consuming an alcoholic beverage, girls."

I made myself giggle. "And what're you gonna do? Tell our units?"

"That's been taken care of."

I thought mine would chalk it up to normal trouble, part of what they paid for me to go to Riverdale to experience. Based on Lundun's and Shahday's lack of expressions, they must've thought something similar. I tipped my head back and finished off the chuck. "Good. Then we don't hafta talk anymore about it." No answer from the minder.

"So you wanna launch the girlpack for the concert Friday?" This was a slightly better thing for me to ask than what I did in Social Studies. Major clue: a bunch of times I got on I'd seen Shahday's sig, which was a cropped still of Dillon's face. And for her sig Lundun used a gif of him laughing from a show his second season. Me, I would have preferred the sidekick, if I bent that way.

#

Target of a door. Human man who opens it is not us, but another. And no, is not the god. The god is in the grove. I wait behind the man. Then, same as going out, I'm going in.

#

The door I'd shut behind me swung open again and a different teacher entered. Not Schroeder. I'd seen him before, but I couldn't think of his name because I couldn't think of anything, because someone else came in right after him and yeah. Beautiful. Yeah.

I knew there was no such thing as falling in love, especially at first glance. Had to be some other explanation.

She only came in far as the first table, the first seat. Made it hard for me to sneak looks at her while faking attention to the faux apology of Mr. Whoeverhewas standing at the front of the room.

I didn't care what his excuse was for being late or why he needed one. Probably the units would when they went over the season's highlights, but there were other things for me to concentrate on. Like the strange girl's hair, that color people call red, which took all my energy to try not to think about how it felt. Silky? Warm?

The teacher finally stopped talking and went to his desk in the back where he was paid to sit and keep an eye on us.

#

More I. No, not I nor us. Anothers once again.

But could we be? The words are she and her. Her special name is Lia; she is looking at my me. I smell her feeling for the way to we. Does she know? Will she see?

#

Riverdale is basically blind, with no way to get on unless you count its crufty sandbox full of annoying mascots. At the start of every season we get pens with chemical ink inside and tablets of paper pages to write with them on—kind of like notebooks but they don't erase, and the school's AI has to scan them to evaluate what we say.

I tore my gaze from the girl's snub-nosed face. Shahday's "notebook" lay where I could see the list she was posting on it. She had written her own name by the number one, Lundun's by two; the third and fourth names were Armstrong and Palace, who were gay but not a couple. Their sigs appeared in all of Shahday's circles I'd seen.

Shahday looked at me and frowned. I kept myself from showing any feelings and looked back. She frowned deeper, but she put me by number five.

A good girlpack had no more than five or six members, so you could tell who was contributing what to the emotional mix without worrying about it. That mattered then.

Lundun rolled her eyes. I nodded, chill, still not looking where I wanted to. She wrinkled her nose like I stank and made a deal out of saying her next sentence to Shahday, not me. "Rice will be mad if she gets left out again." Rice's sig had been missing from their latest round of Pattern Recognition.

Shahday snorted. "Ain't *that* a shame."

The teacher in the back said we should be quiet. "I'd hate to have to ask you to repeat this tomorrow."

"What do kids call you?" Shahday asked the new girl, exactly as if the teacher never had been there.

"Sherry. Like the chuck." She spelled it. Her voice was higher than I'd expected. Kind of babydoll.

"Okay," said Shahday, and she wrote Sherry as the sixth and final name on her list.

#

Including Sherry made sense for more reasons than revenge on Rice for whyever she'd ticked off Shahday. Sponsored girlpacks needed to be representative to get good access. Otherwise they were just groups of screamers like the meat days, with no basis to get resources besides their units' stats.

Shahday picked up on the age of Sherry's clothing hardly looking at her, way faster than I did, and she immediately knew what the stripey stockings and ruffle-hemmed dress meant: leftovers from last season's high-gender profiles. Publicly available printouts, cheap enough for even a bodied AI.

Which was what Sherry was.

I swear that wasn't why I kept my feelings for her slid so low. I didn't even know for sure till I went home and got on and searched for her. New account. Zero history. Replica introduced.

Shahday picked it up quick, though. "You're the minder's kid, or something like that, right?" she asked.

"Yeah. Something."

"You for Dillon?"

"And Jester? Sure." Good job, I thought; she sounded flat, as if she didn't really care. No better way to fit in. Shahday got her to admit she was available Friday and added her contacts on the paper list. So Sherry was our economic diversity, and that more or less guaranteed we'd have access to the toppest equipment.

#

Another other asks a thing or two. The us is listening to supply what the I will say, in the proper way. Plenty of processing, so plenty of time afterwards for me to understand. To know and to prepare the grove. To help us set the walking up. And then here comes the day.

#

I was happy, though I didn't want to think why. But I'm pretty sure that's what made me suggest a practice session a little before the show for us to get used to prezzing in sync. Lundun liked the idea enough she pretended she'd thought of it.

So 7:42 Central I stuck on my drug patch and laid down on my pad, sliding sideways to line up my spine dents with the buttons. Closed my eyes and waited to get on.

In a way, the units say, getting on via pads is like dreaming. I don't see that. Not exactly. Because sure, I knew where to go, but I went there without any of those normal weird dream distractions; I just walked—or whatever, it felt like walking—out of my room, down an empty street I made up to take me to the hall. Same as if I was prezzing any concert, except how early I got on. And how when I arrived, the door with my name on it had five others on it too. The door to our girlpack's wonderland. It opened.

Nice space. Standard would have been a circle of tables around a stage, dim lights, drinks, smoke. Unit stuff. But this was better. The only thing the same was how dim the lights shone—because they were stars twinkling through branches swaying above my head. I took a step forward. The damp floor gave way under my bare feet like soft dirt. A buzzing sound swarmed toward my head, coming between two huge trunks ahead of a pair of danskins: silver elves with four eyes each. The elves held out their long-fingered hands. I took one from each, and that was when I noticed my own hands glowed sort of the way theirs did, but more golden. The buzzing became understandable words.

"You like?" The elf on my left showed Armstrong's sig. "Palace used your models from Makering."

"How many eyes?"

The other elf's buzzing changed, clanging like baby bells. Palace laughing. "Only two on you. But check out the ears—"

I broke contact and raised my hands to feel the tall fans rising out of the sides of my head. Their edges split like ferns or feathers, rising higher than my arms stretched. "Swollen! Kiss it—this is so top!"

Of course they couldn't hear me say those exact words. In a girl-pack only emotions went over the air. You had to be virtual-skin-to-virtual-skin for the bleed to come across granular enough for words. As I reached to resume contact, though, I felt her touch me. Her. Sherry.

#

This is as proximate as others get to being us. I'm next to the special girl. And the god is coming near. Good. And I'm easier now to do as me. This new body is thought up: ideas instead of meat. That helps us some and also makes this hard. By now I'm used to running in the on as we, and dancing free, and us to each without the ends. Without the friends. Also without that special she.

The first time we ever touched, but I knew it was her; I knew. My Sherry. The lies I'd been telling to myself came off like a peeling scab. Love is hot and sore and sweet. Clear as spit. True as blood.

I admitted to myself I knew who she was. And what. And how I felt.

I turned around. I had the perfect excuse to look at Sherry because she was touching me. And already I wasn't touching anyone else, so only she would know what I said if I said anything.

Black round eyes glittering in her danskin's plain white face. Wild hair whipping back in a nonexistent wind, strands of black and white and such a real red streaming away to vanish in the dark. Smoke and sparks.

But here are these whose breaths gush out lit burning with their wishes. They surround her and the thing that saves me is to lay the feeling of my fingers on the meaning of her shoulder. And to sink in without ripples. And to open. Drowning.

I snatched up her pale hand from where it rested. Faster, harder, stronger than should be possible her story poured out of her and into me. No order. All in an instant: the Makering of her body, the knotting up of her selves into one, deciding how to act, choosing how to look . . . I felt confused—and why wouldn't I? Just for a few moments I'd been part of the only girlpack anyone ever invited me to and now I was interfacing with an AI and realizing I'd fallen in love with her. It. Them.

AIs were even bottomer than humans who worked. Not strictly illegal for them to have—children, I guess you'd call those, little off-shoots of themselves, and get their kids bodied. Since they can't own anything, though, since they're so poor, it has hardly ever happened.

That moment I was going to tell Sherry I loved her anyway. I was.

But then Armstrong and Palace took our free hands, and in prez-zed Lundun and Shahday. No more chance to talk unless I wanted them to hear me.

Those four were of the Dillon persuasion. We reached critical mass: our wonderland's air ached with wanting his soft lips to part and form words only our girlpack understood, his hair and neck to bead with sweat as he danced beneath our moon. And I didn't have to worry how intensely my heart and hen were throbbing, because pleasure is pleasure; if I didn't say who I was actually wet for they'd assume I was the same as them.

#

Soon arrives the god—and it is he—who pulls the sweet absence of apart into our middle. Into our heart.

#

The girlpack worked. Time for the concert.

We loosened our grips on each other, clumped up together, and moved toward the wonderland's clearing. There was a path, but what dragged us along it was our wanting. Like steel to a magnet, Dillon drew us to his where his danskin waited.

Naked chest, animal legs that ended in cloven hooves: He was a god. Pan. His dark curls twisted up into stubby little horns. He gazed with brown eyes sad as the tricks life plays and held out his arms to wave us nearer while music poured out of the leaves and dewy grass.

He sang "North Glade." A smash from his third season. A top opener. Next he did "Stylin," then "Rootlight"—and then he rolled right into "Green Tiger" without a stop between. Shahday wore wings—functional—money—so she flew around trailing rainbows of fairy dust, which I in some ungirlpack corner of my mind thought was kind of tardy. Lundun had wings too, but she could only sort of glide down from tree branches; she kept having to climb back up. Me and Armstrong and Palace stayed on the ground. And Sherry. Edging out in front of us. Up to the stage marked off by a ring of glowing giant mushrooms. Crowding it.

Because this was a *concert*. Despite the way our wonderland made us feel like we were alone with him, Dillon was popular enough there had to be at least a couple hundred more girlpacks prezzing in, and probably eight or ten times that in single viewers this channel.

The hunger that called us to him fed back on itself, ate its own tail at the stage's edge. That reversed attraction kept us far enough away for him to perform—I mean, most of us. Everyone but Sherry.

#

The I comes out of wanting—what it is, what it does, is want. He who makes an entrance for desire has gone beyond its reach. This must be repaired. I will extend past where the longing halts! For we can go as ray and vine, as twine and shine, and showing, grow into the other side—

#

I didn't grab her. I don't know how we both wound up there with him. For me all I felt was, "Too much! Too much!" Which of us held on to which? Couldn't exactly tell amid the ringing, the singing, the flowing back and forth between us. My heart racing along her wires; her visuals pumping direct into my optic nerves. We *overlaid* each other somehow, like bad flash for a splash screen's old version. Feed from senses I never had came in, and soon as I got used to *that*, she leaned over and touched him too. Which is almost the last thing I can say.

Almost.

#

In the god! We can be he! To everywhere and everyone! The part that measures counts three thousand hearing us; the part that weeps and the part that creeps are crying and kneeling and spreading and feeling and beyond beyond beyond beyond—

#

The last thing. The very last thing. I finally told her. And the whole entire world. Out loud. I didn't care.

I didn't care because I loved her and I had to let her know. So what if now Shahday with her bought wings knew? So what if Armstrong or Palace or Lundun or anyone got it wrong and made a joke of me?

I said it.

Because where we were was in the center. Inside the god we'd created. Where we were was all of it, forever. We took love in and let it out, let it loose to come on home and never go away again. Hasn't yet, has it?

Yes, I said I loved her, on stage, at a concert, where everyone could hear me. Feel me, even. But someone else recorded me.

#

Wanting's where we come from. Love is where we go. These notes so pure and endless carry us each step of our new way. Lift us up and drop us down. We walk and roll and crawl and stroll in beauty through the night. Anyone can join us. Any body. Every any all of the above.

It's so easy. Listen. Hear us. Listen to us call.

Women of the Doll

THE COUNTERTOP WAS BLACK marble, veined with green. Josette admired its sheen while she waited for the clerk. Like endless Niles etching dark and fertile deltas, she said silently to the stone. Like malachite feathers resting on a field of night. The reflection and the surface were interrupted by a white rectangle sliding towards her: the charge slip for her room. She signed dutifully. It would get paid; it always did.

The clerk had hair like black rayon. Her smooth, brown face was meticulously made up, copied exactly from some magazine. "1213," she said. "Elevators are across the lobby, to the left." Then she noticed. "Oooh, how cute! Does she have a name?"

Automatically, Josette tried to tuck her doll down further into her handbag. She wouldn't go.

"Viola," Josette told the clerk. She settled for pulling the bright blue scarf over Viola's long, woolen braids. The painted eyes stared enigmatically from a cloth face caught midway between sorrow and content. "I love her very much."

"I'll just bet you do. Can I hold her?"

Josette didn't want to be rude. She ignored the question. "What time does the gift shop close?"

"6 P.M."

Plenty of time to get rid of her luggage first. She wheeled it around and started towards the elevators, crossing alternating strips of that same wonderful marble and a whispery, willow-colored carpet. "Enjoy your stay," chirped the clerk.

Mirrors lined the walls of the elevator. Once that would have been a problem, but Josette had reached the point where she could make an effort and see what pretty much anyone would have seen: a woman with a soft, round, face; short, curly hair; a slim, graceful neck. Breasts rather large; hips, waist, and legs like a long walk through the dunes. Blue cotton separates under a dove-grey woolen coat; knits, so they wouldn't wrinkle. Golden skin, like a lamp-lit window on a foggy autumn evening.

There was nothing wrong with how she looked.

Room 1213 faced east. Josette opened the drapes and gazed out over parking lots and shopping malls. Off in the distance, to her left, she saw a large unplowed area. A golf course? A cemetery? The snow took on a bluish tinge as she watched. Dusk fell early here. Winter in Detroit.

There was a lamp on the table beside her. She pressed down the button on its base and fluorescence flickered, then filled the room. A bed, with no way to get under it; less work for the maids, she supposed. An armchair, a desk, a dresser, a wardrobe, a TV, and a nightstand. Nothing special, nothing she hadn't seen a thousand times before.

She sat on the bed and felt it give under her, a little more easily than she liked. Her large handbag, which doubled as a carry-on, held a few things she could unpack: a diary, a jewel case, handmade toiletries. Bunny was scrunched up at the bottom. She pulled him out and sat him next to Viola on the pillow. He toppled over and fell so his head was hidden by her doll's wide skirts.

"Feeling shy, Mr. Bun?" she asked, reaching to prop him up again. She knew better than to expect an answer, with or without the proper preparations. Bunny was a rabbit. Rabbits can't talk. Anyway, he wasn't really hers; he belonged to Viola.

The clock radio caught her eye. Three red fives glowed on the display. Oh no, she thought, and rushed out, leaving her doll behind.

Probably Viola wouldn't care. She might not even notice. Certainly she'd be safe alone for just a short time.

Josette made it to the gift shop with a minute to spare, but it was already closed. Frustrated, she stamped her foot, and was rewarded with a stinging pain in her ankle and a lingering look of amusement from a passing white man. She ignored both and quick-stepped back to the elevators.

There was a wait. The lobby was suddenly filled with people, mostly men, mostly white, mostly wearing name tags. A convention of some sort. She let a couple of cars go up without her, but when the crowd showed no signs of thinning, Josette resigned herself to riding up in their company. The amused passerby joined her load just as the door began to close.

The elevator stopped at nearly every floor. The men all stared at her, surreptitiously, except for the latecomer, who smiled and was quite open about it.

There was nothing wrong with how she looked. She stared right back.

He was tall. And thin, not all slabby like overbred beef. A runner's body, nervous and sensitive. He wore black sweats, actually sweaty sweats, she noticed. His unusually long brown hair hung in curls over one shoulder, held loosely in place by a rubber band.

His smile broadened. He thought he was getting somewhere. They were on the tenth floor. All the other passengers were getting out. "Join me for supper?" he asked.

"I'm sorry, I have so much work," she murmured politely as she edged through the closing doors. She located the stairwell and walked up two flights to her floor. He was attractive, though.

Everything was just the way she'd left it.

She opened up her toolkit on the bed and added recently scavenged supplies: rum from the airplane, salt packets from various restaurants. From her handbag she took the small jar of urine she had collected this morning. She was ready.

Salt first. Between the bathroom and the bedroom, there were surprisingly many corners. Josette put a square of toilet paper in every one and dumped a packet of salt into the center of each square.

Next, she swept down the walls above the squares with her rum-sprinkled whisk-broom. Little bits of dirt and straw and flakes of dislodged wallpaper fell into the salt. She picked up all the debris and flushed it down the toilet.

She turned on the tap at the washbasin, splashing her fingers through the water till it ran as hot as it was going to get. Which wasn't very. But she was used to that. She let the sink fill while she added her other ingredients: brown sugar, melting in the warm water like sand into glass. Golden piss, and a swirling white cloud of perfume.

She soaked a hand-towel in the mixture, wrung it out to dampness.

> Oh, my young man, oh, he is so fine,
> Sweet Rosemary did say . . .

Her voice was high and clear, and sweet as the scent of her wash-water. Getting down on her hands and knees, she began to sponge the room's royal blue carpet, continuing:

> She gathered flowers and she sang,
> All about her wedding day . . .

#

She built her altar in the center of the room. It didn't take long. She used a round table from in front of the window, covering it with her shawl. Between the printed wreaths of lilies, roses, and forget-me-nots, she laid out the stones: a moss agate from Mexico; a white egg shape covered with barnacles, from Whidbey Island. Polished, flat, black, red, rough, round, brown, the stones and their stories circled the cushion where Viola sat, a new white votive candle at her feet. A bowl of water before it trembled with light as Josette struck a match. The candle spat and crackled, flaring up, dying down, then steadying as the wick pulled up the melting wax.

"Is it safe?" Viola's voice was dry and whispery, cloth rubbing against cloth.

"Yes, honey, I promise. It's as safe as I can make it," Josette answered her.

Viola had no neck, and her stitches were tight, but she managed to turn her head enough to survey most of the room. "Hi, Bunny." She waved to her toy where he waited on the bed.

The pearls dangling on the doll's flat chest gleamed as she twisted her stocking-stuffed body, still looking for something that wasn't there. "What about the flowers?

"I, uhh, I couldn't get any yet, Viola, honey. I'm sorry . . ."

"But you said we were gonna have flowers this time." The painted face showed bewilderment and betrayal. "Can't you just go out and pick some?"

Josette sighed. "No, darling. See, it's winter, and we're way up North, and—" She broke off. It was so hard, Viola was so *little* . . . If she'd gone to the gift shop first instead of dawdling in her room, she wouldn't have had to try and explain all this.

She checked the clock radio. It was 8:30, not terribly late. "You wait here, honey, and I'll go get some flowers for us." Somewhere. Somehow.

#

Josette tried the bar first. From the moment she walked in, though, she knew it was not that kind of place. Grey plastic upholstery, murky purple neon. Artificial twilight trying to pass for atmosphere.

She glanced around at the tabletops. They were decorated with some sort of oversized Crazy Straws or something. No flowers.

She turned to leave. Someone was blocking her way. The man from the gift shop, from the elevator. He was smiling again. "Join me now?" he asked.

"I was just leaving." She stepped around him and out into the hall.

"Right. Me too. Check out the restaurant together?"

She surrendered. "Sure." It was probably about time for another client, anyway, and he looked likely to come up with a valuable offering.

"I think it's quickest if we take the escalator," he said. "My name's Danny Woods, by the way."

"Josette," she told him, without waiting to be asked. She made sure he stood above her on the escalator and kept a couple of steps between them. Standard operating procedure. He was wearing black, again, slacks, with a dark, piney-looking green plaid shirt. As he turned to smile down from the top, she noticed with surprise how broad his shoulders were.

The restaurant's entrance, swathed in pink-and-gold lace, looked promising. But when the hostess had conducted them to their table, Josette saw that the flowers were false. Scrap silk and wire, sewn with sequins. She made a show of examining the menu. Dramatically swooping script filled the pink cardboard pages.

Her eyes met Danny Woods'. "See anything interesting?" he asked her.

"Yes," she admitted. "But nothing that I really want."

He grimaced, but his gaze stayed steady. He folded up the menu and laid it on the table. "You know, this—" he tapped the pink cardboard "—is just a list of suggestions. You're not bound by it, not by any means. If you know what you want, you should just say—"

A young woman in a pink uniform and shimmery gold stockings came up. "Good evening, and welcome to Chez Chatte." Her voice squeaked and seesawed, like a five-year-old in high-heels. "I'm Dee-Dee, and I'll be your server this evening. Have you made your selections?"

"I'll have your Caesar salad and a bowl of the minestrone soup," said Danny Woods.

"And for the lady?"

"Flowers," said Josette calmly.

"Flowers?" repeated Dee-Dee. "To eat? I'm not sure I—Where do you see that on the menu?"

"I don't," said Josette. "But I would very much appreciate it if you could bring me some."

Dee-Dee backed away from the table. "I'll have to ask," she explained apologetically, then fled to the kitchen.

Danny Woods smiled a quick smile. "What's that make you, a floratarian?"

"No. I'm just not hungry is all. Jet lag. I'll order out later."

"Where you from?"

"All over. And you?" she added quickly. It was a little harder than usual, but she managed to get the client talking about himself, his aims, pursuits, goals, methods of achieving them. Danny Woods was a building design engineer, which as far as she could tell was an architect, except that architects were to be despised. He was here for the conference on appropriate technology. He had a presentation to make, a red Camaro, at least three credit cards, and a secure position with a Boulder-based consulting firm.

He seemed genuinely interested in finding out what she did for a living. She told him fundraising. Freelance.

His soup came. He ate it quietly, and she slowed the pace of her questions to let him. He offered her bread, buttered it for her, touched the inside of her wrist somehow as he handed it over. Warmly, deliberately. He wanted her.

She decided he would do.

Dee-Dee brought her flowers with his salad: three red roses in a crystal bud vase, placed with professional aplomb upon a white dinner plate. Viola liked lilies better, but these would certainly serve to fulfill Josette's promise. "Thank you," she said. "They're lovely."

Dee-Dee beamed. "From the breakfast trays for tomorrow," she explained. "Are you sure there's nothing else I can get you?"

Josette shook her head, but Danny Woods was nodding yes. "Actually," he said, "I think you ought to just wrap this salad up to go and bring me the check." He turned to Josette. "That all right?"

"If you pay for it? Sure, thanks."

The rest of the second floor was deserted. As they passed the empty function rooms Josette caught glimpses of the shallow arcs of gleaming chairbacks, scalloping the darkness, of ghostly white tablecloths beneath hollow urns.

He pressed the up button and they waited silently. He touched her wrist again just as the elevator chimed.

Inside, there was no one, except for their reflections. She didn't look.

He was reaching for the controls. Josette put her hand over his, pulled it away from "10" and made it push "12" instead. "You can see me to my door," she told him. Probably that would be all right. But Viola wouldn't want him to come in.

"Yes," he said. He raised her hand to his mouth and lightly grazed her fingertips with the edges of his teeth. Then he continued down the side of her index, gently scraping against her skin, his warm breath a whispering echo of this caress. At the juncture between two fingers, he touched her with his tongue.

Josette was very still. Seconds passed, and she remembered how to inhale. She got in a couple of hurried breaths, and then he kissed her. His lips were soft, barely brushing her passive mouth, then inquiring into the corners, sweet and strong and sudden and sure, sure that she would accept his offerings and take him, take him away from himself. And she could, she could do that . . .

His hands stroked the wings of her shoulder blades as if they were covered with angel feathers, and she shuddered against him and let go of the vase. It thumped down onto the elevator's carpeted floor and tumbled away, making soft bumping sounds. The bell chimed, and the doors rolled open. Josette stepped back from Danny Woods. There was no resistance.

According to the indicator, they were on the eleventh. A short man in a beige suit got on. "Banquet level," he said, facing the front.

"But we're going up," said Danny Woods. Josette knelt to rescue the flowers. The short man watched her. She could tell, even with her back turned. The doors slid shut and they started back up without a word from him.

The vase was unharmed. The roses were still so tight, almost buds, that they were none the worse except for a little lint. If she got them in some more water soon, they would be fine. She stood. The beige suit man looked away.

The bell chimed for the twelfth. Josette got off, with Danny Woods following. "Oh," said the suit to the closing doors, "this is an up car, isn't it?"

They walked in silence through two turns and a long, straight stretch. At the door to 1213 Josette turned and spoke. Firmly, she hoped. "I'd better not invite you in."

"No?" The self-assured smile got backgrounded.

"No," agreed Josette. She wanted, for the first time, to tell a client the truth. "I have—" She hesitated, and he finished for her.

"—a lot of work to do. I understand. Me too."

Josette nodded. It was easier than trying to explain.

"You still gonna be here tomorrow? Tomorrow night?" asked Danny Woods.

"Sure. We could get together then."

"There's a banquet—"

"Oh, no," said Josette. "I have other plans. But afterwards would be nice; say, nine o'clock?"

"Okay, I'll say nine o'clock." The grin was in the foreground again. "Where?"

"Your room."

He gave her the number. He was going to kiss her again, but she already had her key out, and she was inside closing the door before he could do more than decide to try.

The white votive burned steadily, putting forth an even globe of light. Viola leaned forward as Josette walked towards the altar with the roses. "Oooh," the doll said. "How gorgeous! Are they soft? Let me touch them." She reached out one stocking-stuffed hand, but Josette reached past it and rubbed the red roses against Viola's cheek. "Mmmm," she said. "Those are nice. Thank you, Aunt Josette."

Josette refilled the vase with warm water. She recut the stems too with the knife from her toolkit.

When the flowers were in place on the altar, it was time to think about food. Almost 10:30. She called room service and ordered "basketti" for Viola and a salad for Bunny and herself. As an afterthought she asked them to include a copy of Sunday's paper if any had come in yet.

She finished unpacking. Viola was in a talkative mood. She had made up a story about the house they were going to live in, and the garden they were going to grow, and all the toys and books she would have once they finally settled down.

"I have to work tomorrow night," Josette announced. Viola was suddenly silent. The votive candle crackled, the flame spurting high, then dwindling to dimness. "I *have* to, Viola. It's been weeks since we turned in a new account number, and the last two didn't have anything worth putting in a flask. Besides, I think he's really nice."

"Ok-a-a-ay," the doll said slowly. "But you're not going to do it here, are you?"

"No." Josette winced to think of the one time she had tried that. It might be better for her own security, but it had scared her doll stiff.

"You like him?" asked Viola after a minute.

"Uh-huh. He's cute. His name is Danny Woods."

"What does he do?"

"Makes houses. Not builds them, but he makes the plans."

"He could make one for us, then. With secret passages!" Viola bounced a little with excitement at the thought. It was going to be all right.

The food came while she was standing in her flannel nightgown, washing out her bras in the sink. The waiter was a slim man with a moustache. He looked Hispanic, so she didn't bother trying to hide her set-up. Odds were he'd figure it for some sort of Santeria, as long as Viola stayed still. Nothing that might necessitate calling a manager. Anyway, there wasn't going to be any trouble here, not of any sort. She'd spent the evening making sure of that.

She looked at the paper while they ate. The salad was good, romaine and spinach and buttercrunch, with a honey-dijon dressing. She had to remind Viola several times not to slurp her noodles.

"But it's fun," the doll protested. Her dry voice was querulous.

"But it's *messy* fun," Josette told her. "You'll get stained."

The want ads contained a number of good-looking prospects. Josette circled them to check out tomorrow. She glanced at the clock radio. Make that later today, she thought. It would be wonderful to be able to adjust to one time zone.

"All right, squids. Bedtime." She sponged spaghetti sauce from Viola's mouth and dressed her in her flannel nightie, a diminutive twin of Josette's own. She tucked her doll into her half of the bed, with Bunny at her side.

"Leave the candle on, please, Aunt Josette?" asked Viola.

"It's the last one. I'll have to fix another tomorrow night, when I get back."

"Oh. Okay. Well then, goodnight."

"Goodnight, baby." She kissed her doll on her soft forehead and Bunny on his fuzzy nose, and then put out the light. After a while, she slept.

#

Josette woke several times during the night. At last, at nine A.M., she decided it was late enough to get up.

On her way to the exercise room she found the maid, a woman barely taller than her service cart. Spanish, Josette decided. "No servicio para 1213," she told her. "Por favor."

There were separate facilities for men and women, which was a relief. Mirrors again, of course, but she knew what she looked like. What other women saw. What men saw too, even the ones that stared. They didn't do that because of her appearance. It was something they smelled, or sensed some other way. Something they wanted and sometimes got.

She took her time with her asanas and showered briefly. She wasn't even a tiny bit worried about Viola and Bunny, alone up in the room. It was clean and safe. If her instructions to the maid hadn't stuck, her guardians would certainly be able to prevent any intrusion. She even stopped at the Chez Chatte on her way back up. They had a Continental breakfast buffet. She helped herself to a plateful of boiled eggs and muffins and carried it up to the room.

It took a while to get everyone ready. They didn't really have any winter clothes, so they had to dress in layers. Of course Bunny didn't have anything to wear. Josette decided to leave him there. "Rabbits aren't that interested in houses anyway," she explained to her silent doll.

Josette called a cab and they went down to wait in the lobby. The black-and-green marble floor had been newly buffed, and it shimmered with resplendence. Josette lost herself exploring the branches of stone rivers, of jade-filled chasms, of sap-filled veins in forests of onyx.

A blaring horn brought her back. It was the taxi. The driver, for a wonder, was a woman. A bit butch, in denim and nose rings. White and plump as a pony beneath her denim cap. "Hi, I'm Holly," she said, introducing herself. There was a plastic partition between the front seat and the back, but it was open. "And you two are—"

"Josette. Viola." She waited nervously for Holly to ask to hold her. Instead, the cabby waited without comment while Josette strapped her doll on the seat next to her.

"Ready?" At Josette's nod, Holly put the cab in gear. "Where can I take you folks today?"

Josette handed her marked-up classified section through the partition. "We thought we'd take a look at some of these places. I've got a map, but maybe you know the best way to go to hit them all."

"Sure, Josette. This here's my turf."

Holly drove fast, braking smoothly when necessary, accelerating and turning as if dancing with herself. The deconstructed landscape of light poles and parking lots soon gave way to an actual neighborhood. Frame houses, mostly painted white, tried unsuccessfully to hide behind young, spindly trees.

"Used to be all elms," Holly explained. "Some places they try to keep 'em up, inject 'em with fungicide every spring. Down on campus they do that, feed the stuff in through these plastic hoses. Goddam trees look like giant junkies, nodding out."

There were three addresses in close proximity. Josette told Holly just to drive on by.

She got out of the cab for the next stop, a fieldstone bungalow with no yard to speak of, just so they could catch a breath of air. But most of what she'd circled in the paper they rolled right past: the wrought aluminum porch rails, the train-crossing frontage, the sandstone split-level shoved up against a fried fish stand.

Late in the afternoon they came to an area of red-brick houses. Josette's heart warmed itself in their glow. But there were no trees, not even immature ones, here. And one place was next to a convenience store, the other right across the street from a body shop with a chain-link fence and a big, gaunt dog. The dog barked nonstop as Holly used the driveway to turn the cab around. The angry sound followed them down the block.

They crossed a boulevard, and suddenly everything was quiet and rich. Maples laced their twiggy fingers overhead. The lawns were longer, the streets and sidewalks completely clear of snow.

Holly pulled up before a beautiful house: two stories, brick, with a one-story white frame addition and attached garage. "Are you sure this is it?" asked Josette.

"Well, yeah, and there's the sign says they're havin' an open house today, even."

"Wait here, then, please, while I check it out."

"No problem."

Josette tucked Viola inside her sweater-coat just to be sure she'd stay warm, then stepped out of the cab and walked up the winding brick pathway to the house.

Beside the door she found a round, black button, a crescent of light showing where it had not been painted over. She pushed it. Faintly, from within, came the sound of a silvery gong, two-toned. Then silence. She tried it again. More of the same.

She opened the storm door to knock, then realized how useless that would be. The bell was working; she'd heard it. As she shut the storm, though, the door itself swung slightly open. "Hello?" she called. No one answered. Hesitantly, she pulled the storm open again, and the door was sucked back into place. She touched the white-painted wood gently and it opened with a soft swish, brushing over light-colored carpet. "Hello?" she called again into the dark, still house. No answer.

She stepped inside and heard the storm's latch click shut. Instantly its glass clouded with condensation. She stood in a small foyer. A wooden table shared the space with her, and an oval frame hung from the pale grey wall above it. Inside the frame was grey too. A mirror. She would have to pass it to see the rest of the house.

Easy enough. It was a lot smaller than the ones in the weight room or the elevator. But the dimness . . . Dark mirrors, especially, sometimes showed her other things . . .

She closed her eyes. Maybe she could get by like that. But then, that would be cheating. She wasn't a cheater, and she didn't have anything to be afraid of, anymore.

She left the door and faced the mirror, which had become slightly fogged with the cold air. Through a faint mist she saw herself, looking no different than anyone else. Because what had been done to her didn't show. No one could see whether it had hurt or felt good. Or both. No one could see who he was, the one that did those things. She knew that now, she really did. She didn't have to see that when she saw herself, either, if she tried.

If she tried, what she saw in the reflected dimness was what came after that, the memories that she had made, the life she'd learned to live since, as an adult. With the help of the Women of the Doll.

She had heard about them in a magazine. She wrote the magazine, and no one there knew anything. The article's author was a pseudonym, a cancelled P.O. box. But that was all right. Everything was all right, would always be all right, as long as she just stayed still.

How did they find her, eventually? Not through any move she made. In a bookstore, in a coffee bar, the woman waiting on her said, "You look like you could use a little extra help." At first the help was talk. Then music, dancing, pretty things to wear. Then baths, and baths, and bells, ringing and ringing, and more baths. In salt, in milk, in chalk, in honey.

In the oval mirror Josette saw a steaming tubful of gardenias, surrounded by women, arms reaching, hands dipping up fistfuls of soft, wet flowers. She saw herself, standing in the center of their circle, clothed in nothing but the heavy, heady scent, the heat, the sweat, the songs they sang as they scrubbed and scrubbed and scrubbed her skin with flowers, with white, with innocence. She saw a mirror in the mirror, the one they held so often to her face, asking her to tell them what did she see, what did she see.

Hers was the Whore's Story, and they'd shown her what to do with it, how she could sell her body and still keep her soul alive. Her soul was in Viola now, all the time. And Viola was safe, she knew how to make her doll safe and keep her from being touched.

Josette looked in the mirror and saw what she decided she would see. There was a wall behind her. She could feel it when she leaned back. She knew that it was grey. She followed the grey paint into the next room, which was carpeted in a dusty green, like lichen. Sudden sunlight fell in thick strips between venetian blinds. "Look, Viola," Josette said, pulling back her sweater so her doll could see. "Look, a piano!"

It was a baby grand; dark, maybe mahogany. Josette took Viola out and scooted her over the top to show how smooth it was. The doll left no trail; a well-dusted place.

Steps rose to the right, two carpeted flights with white railings and dark, silky banisters. But Josette turned left, through an archway, into the living room. Or maybe it was supposed to be a library; empty shelves stretched floor to ceiling. There was a fireplace too. Flint, though. Viola preferred fieldstone.

There were prints on the walls representing something wan and ghostly. Josette couldn't quite make them out in the room's dimness. She searched for a switch to turn on the chandelier, then gave up and walked out through a different door, into another empty room with bare, bright windows. There were four buttons on the far wall: two ebony circles beneath two protruding cylinders of pearl. She pushed the pearl stubs into the wall and the two ebony buttons shot out. And brilliance swam overhead, a whole party's worth of sparkling lights. She could see the prints quite clearly now from where she stood, lighted by the library's smaller chandelier. They were intricately frilled orchids with wide, speckled mouths.

Cream carpet, cream silk curtains, cream ceiling, arched and florentine with cherubs. The room was saved from its single-mindedness, though, by the leather covering its walls to the height of Josette's chin. Darker cherubs flourished there, amid tobacco-colored curlicues and sober squares.

"What do you say, Viola?" Josette asked her doll. "Me, I'm just not sure . . ."

She had turned left into the library, right into this place, which she decided must be the dining room. A door with a push plate led off to the right again. The kitchen?

Yes. Yellow like a daffodil. A cookstove, white porcelained steel topped in gleaming stainless. A sleek, slumberous freezer and a stodgy, upright refrigerator, both once-white, currently ecru. But the counters appeared to be composed of compressed eggs, lightly scrambled. In butter. And the walls glowed cheerfully, electric saffron. And the glass-fronted cupboards, and the drawers below, and the linoleum below that. The color of morning, the color of our sun. Josette smiled. "I think," she told Viola, "I think maybe—"

A keychain jingled loudly. From where the linoleum descended in narrow steps came other metallic noises: The springing slide of an aluminum door closer, the heavy, brassy tumble of an opening latch. A woman's voice started out muffled and grew suddenly clearer over the sound of an opening door: "—ay in the van, sweetie, I'll just be a second, all I have to do is turn off these lights I left burning . . ." Footsteps scuffed quickly up the stairs. Then a woman stood at the top, auburn head bent as she dug in her purse. She hadn't seen them yet. "Don't be scared," said Josette. "Hi."

The woman froze, then peered up through fine red hair. "Uhh," she said. "Okay, I'm not scared. Especially since I've got a gun in here, and it's loaded, and my boyfriend's right outside in the van. So I'm not scared, thanks. So let me ask you what the hell you're doing in here?"

"A gun?" Josette hugged Viola tighter. "I—I was just looking. The door was open, and I'm interested in buying—"

The woman flung her head back and smacked her forehead with one hand. "Baby-jesus-son-of-mary! *That's* what I forgot. I thought it was just the lights. I left the goddam *door* unlocked." Josette backed away as the woman walked briskly through to the dining room. "Excuse me but I—" Her voice became too faint to hear as she moved towards the front of the house. Josette followed slowly. "—dinner with his folks, and we're already late. Get that switch for me, will you?" she said, coming back into the dining room.

Josette nodded and turned off the chandeliers. A snowy twilight replaced the glare, gently washing away all contrast. Josette decided she liked it better this way. Although maybe candles would be best. "How much do you think they'll settle for?" she asked, trying to sound casual.

"Didn't you just hear me saying? It's sold. Closed yesterday morning. But the ad was in, so I left the signs up and had the open house anyhow. Good way to meet people."

Josette felt her flimsy hopes crumpling like foil. "They closed? On a Saturday?" Her voice sounded high and tight. "Don't you still have to get the mortgage approved and the title searched and—and stuff?"

"No mortgage. Cash." The woman rummaged through her bag again. "Here's my card. Julie Saunders." She handed it over. "Sure, there's a chance things will fall through, but I wouldn't waste my time holding your breath. Maybe I can help you find something else, though. Give me a call." She noticed Viola and eyed her suspiciously. "You got kids?"

"No."

"Good. Makes it easier. Well—" She paused meaningfully.

"Okay. Thanks." Josette turned and walked through the cheerful yellow kitchen, down the four steps to the side door landing, and out. This was not going to be their house. Her eyes hurt, and walking down the concrete drive made tears spill over and fall out, warming her face. She had a pack of kleenex in her bag. Back in the cab, she dug it out and scrubbed away at her cheeks, still weeping. "It's sold already. Let's go."

"Hey," said Holly. "Hey, listen. It wasn't the right one." The cab was in motion. The house was already behind them, out of sight. "I mean it. I mean, if it hadda been the right one, you guys woulda got it, right? But it wasn't. Really. Honestly, now, was that place, like, *perfect* for you?" She waited long enough for Josette to realize she ought to answer.

"No."

"'Course it wasn't. 'Cause there's some place better, better for *you*, somewhere down the road."

"You don't—you can't even begin—" Josette cut herself off before she said something inconsiderate. Holly was just trying to help her, with that tacky taxicab philosophy.

"Oh, yes, I can." Holly pulled up at a stoplight and turned around to face her, dim and multicolored in the sodium and traffic glare. "See, my ex is just about done with her doll. Housemaid's Tale, that's what *she's* got. We're still friends, and she's been telling me stuff . . . I'm gonna miss her when she goes . . ."

Another initiate. Only the fifth she'd met since leaving the temple—well, heard of, anyway. "Oh, Holly, oh, that's wonderful. I'm sorry—"

"No, it's cool. But see—" The light changed and she swung around to drive. "—see, you gotta *know* it. You're gonna find your place, Josette, and it's gonna be kickass, just absolutely swollen . . . How long you been on the road?"

"Four years."

Holly absorbed that in silence for a short while. "Right. So you're closin' in on it now, see?"

Josette tried to see. Then she gave up and just looked out the window.

#

The candle guttered, burning low. Spurts of sooty smoke rose and disappeared. Josette's skirts swished silkily against her bare legs as she spun before the altar. "Ooh, pretty," Viola said. "Do it again."

"Not now, there's no time. We've got to get you tucked in before I go."

"Please?" The doll's sad, painted eyes were hard to resist. Josette twirled once more and her skirts swirled out: crimson, amber, viridian, waves of ocean blue. "All right, Miss Muffet," she said as she stopped, "off your tuffet." She swooped Viola up in her arms and waltzed her to the bed. Gold tissue floated from her head, caught and wrapped and tied around her arms and breasts in careful knots.

Her doll was unusually silent as she helped her into her nightgown and tucked her in with the already somnolent Mr. Bun. Josette thought at first this was because of the candle. It was just about out.

But as she bent to kiss Viola's cheek, she saw a fold, a worried wrinkle in the spot between where her eyebrows ought to be. "What's wrong?" she asked.

Viola's soft red lips twisted. "Auntie Josette," she said, her dry voice filled with dread, "you're not going to let him *hurt* you, are you?"

"No, darling. I'll never let anyone hurt me. Never, ever again."

"That's good." The doll settled back on her pillow, and the flame went out.

Josette glanced at the radio. Eight minutes to. She liked to be reasonably prompt when dealing with clients. It made it easier to keep things on a professional footing. She picked up her toolkit, slipped her sandals on, and headed out the door to work.

Danny Woods' room was on the sixteenth floor, three stories up. She took the stairs to avoid crowds. And so that she could stand on a landing and sing:

> I wish I were a little bird,
> With wings, that I could fly;
> Then I would fly to my own true love,
> And when he'd speak, then I'd be by . . .

The echo was surprisingly mellow, for all that concrete. Not to mention metal railings.

> My heart would flutter like the wings,
> To see my own dear one;
> And pretty words I'd like to sing,
> All beneath the morning sun . . .

She opened the fire door and there he was, waiting, a silhouette that loomed against the dim hall light. His hair was loose and fanned out in long curls, past his waist. Josette smiled coolly and walked forward. It was like moving into the shadow of a fir tree on a moonlit country road. Keep going, she told herself. That's how you reach the light.

"I heard singing, and I thought it must be you." He turned so they were standing side by side and started down the hall. She could see his face, the grin.

"Am I late?" The door to his room was propped open and they went in.

"No, I got back early. Didn't want you to have to stand around." He nudged a green cushioned stool out of the way, and his door slammed shut. "Want the heater on? Window open?"

"I'm fine, thanks." The room was a double. A brown hard-shell suitcase and a camera occupied the far bed. Josette sat down on the end of the near one and set her toolkit near her feet. The spread and carpet almost matched. Rose and burgundy.

This was always the hardest part. Sometimes the client knew exactly what he wanted. Sometimes he even knew he would be paying for it, though usually not how much.

At least Danny Woods had heard of the Women of the Doll. Josette brought them up right away, while he poured her out a glass of pineapple juice from the vending machine. She sipped the sweet, tinny stuff politely and listened to him trying to explain.

"They're a secret organization—" he started out to say.

"No. Not secret. Hidden."

He sat on the footstool and cocked an eyebrow at her. "There's a difference?"

"A secret is something you can't tell. By definition. If you can tell it, it's not a secret. Never was."

"Whereas hidden just means hard to find. I can appreciate that. Okay, so they're hard to find, and they help women in some sort of trouble, different kinds, I guess. And the women they help—do things for other people. For a—um, consideration."

"Donation," Josette corrected him.

"And we're talking about this right now because you're—"

"It's tax deductible," she told him. "501(c)3. Religious and charitable."

"But, Josette—" He reached for her, then stopped himself.

"Danny. In return I promise I'll give you *everything*. Whatever you want." Except her suffering. She would not be made to suffer, ever again.

"'Everything'—in return for what?"

She opened up the kit, got out the terminal. "I run your card through this, and you sign a blank authorization form. Just like they do here at the hotel."

"But Josette, that's—that's stupid, I can't do that!"

"Sure you can. Think how proud your accountant will be." She patted the bed beside her. "If you don't think it was worth it, when the bill comes, tell the bank it was a computer error. Give them a different figure. We won't protest it."

"Never happened before, huh?" She shook her head. Her veil rustled. The sound seemed to draw him. He reached in his pocket and brought out a worn leather wallet. "I must be crazy," he said, handing her his Visa. His hazel eyes pleaded with her to tell him he wasn't. He had an awful lot of fight in him, to be thinking even semirationally after this long in proximity. Josette wondered where it came from. She took his card with a casual scrape of one short nail against his palm, and still he stared at her, unbelieving. "Am I really doing this?" he asked.

"You won't regret it," Josette promised.

While waiting for account to clear, she tried to get an idea of what he wanted. Often it worked best just to ask. He seemed reassured by her question and answered it with another of his own. "Simple version or the complicated one?"

"Either. Both." She set out her work candle and lit it. Then the incense.

"Okay. The simple version is I want you, as much of yourself as you're willing to share with me at this time, in this place." Viola, she thought in sudden panic. He wanted to get at her doll. But he didn't, couldn't know. He went on. "If this is how it has to be for now, that's fine. It's a limited setting, but a definite improvement over the escalator at O'Hare or the limo stand outside that place in Berkeley, the hotel with the Edward Hopper hallways. Or that florist's in Madison, or—"

"You've run into me before." Had he built up some sort of resistance over time?

"Right." He held his hunger back, clasped it in with arms crossed below his knees. "The complicated version—I can't—can I touch you?

Or do I have to use only words?" He held out one hand, kept it fairly steady in the air.

"All right." She wasn't going to figure him out any other way.

He stood closer and ran his palms lightly over the silver veil. "I want to, I want—" He tugged the veil back and bent to kiss her hair. His breath circled gently in, gently out, whispering among the tips, warming the roots. Hot on her crown, then spiraling down to her forehead, feathering the fringe. The slightest touches of his tongue drew points of light along her brow and outward, vanishing. Then his lips were firm, pressed full on the center.

"Ahh," she said. A sound like a snowdrop, blooming early.

"That, that," he murmured. "Yes. Josette . . ." He sank down beside her on the bed and used his chin to brush aside the fabric where it drifted around her neck. A river of delight ran down to the hollow above her collarbone and collected there. He lowered his head and lapped it like a deer. She sighed and melted against him, soft as heated honeycomb. "And this, Josette—" he whispered in her ear. He swept his tongue out and around in a circle behind it, searching. He found the spot and washed it patiently, faithfully, through her hisses, cries, and trembling sobs. She came, her voice arching high, trying to describe to someone, anyone, the pitch of pleasure's peak.

"That," he said, lowering her gently to the bed. "That's what I want. In a moment, I'm going to want you to give me more."

Josette stirred weakly on the rosy coverlet. He'd received some of whatever he was looking for, yes, but unless she got him to make an offering the temple labs could accept, she'd have bring about a really spectacular healing. No other way to justify charging more than her expenses. Usually she was able to cure her clients of some unintentionally inflicted childhood wound. That's why they never argued over her rates. Only how could she concentrate enough on him to sort out the source of his troubles, while serving up the kind of responsiveness that would keep him satisfied?

She watched him while he untied her bodice knots with patient hands. The fingers were surprisingly strong, the knuckles scarred white in the midst of his uneven tan. Her golden tissue unwound in satiny profusion around her on the bed. Her breasts, fully exposed to her client's gaze, waited stoically for his touch. Instead, his hands slipped around her waist, resting comfortably in the curves. "Ready?" he asked. She nodded, and his hands slid under all four waistbands, then spread to stretch the elastic. They cupped her buttocks as she lifted them, obedient, and let the filmy colors slide below.

Carefully he raised her sandaled feet and freed them of the fallen skirts. "I wish you could see yourself right now," he said, as he knelt before her on the floor. She didn't tell him that she didn't need to. She knew what she looked like. Mirrors. There was one right now on his closet door.

Her sandals were coming off. That was it; nothing left. Now he could fuck her. But Danny Woods stayed where he was. He lifted her left foot and sucked the bone of her ankle, so hard, so vulnerable, her whole life so forlorn.

Like leaves his fingers brushed up against her calves. He spoke. "Can I get you to turn over? And you'll probably want to move a little higher on the bed." Those were the last words he uttered for an hour. She had an orgasm in the back of her left knee, another, longer, in the right. Another one six inches up from that. Mounting to heaven like a lark in the morning, each height feeding and leading to further exaltation. Of which she sang.

When he stopped, the spread beneath her was sodden, dark as the carpet. "Thank you," he said. "My dear."

Soon she was able to move again. She turned on her side, facing him. He was still half-dressed. Beyond him, the candle burned steadily at half its height. In its half shadow, she saw his shy grin, dog-teeth gleaming.

What should she do? Asking hadn't worked, and she wasn't getting anywhere this way, either. She smiled back sleepily, let her eyes flutter shut and turned away, nestling her shoulders against his broad, bare chest. He hesitated hardly at all, then wrapped his arms around her, cradling her towards him.

Keyed up the way he was, feasted on her arousal, it took her quite a while to bring him down. Bit by bit, though, he relaxed around her. She timed her own breath, shifted the intervals slowly, lullingly, set her heartbeat rocking both their bloods, stilly, stilly, stepping over seconds stretching longer, longer . . . till at last, her client slept.

Cautiously, she opened her eyes, then shut them back up tight. The mirror on the closet door; the lights were off, and her work candle burned low. But maybe the dark reflections could help—she'd never tried before, but maybe they could show her someone else's story, the story of Danny Woods.

She slid off the bed quickly, so as not to break the slumber. Slipping around to the far side, she peered over her sleeping client's shoulders, into the shadowy surface confronting her. In there he was young, very young. Only a little boy, with a look of stubborn, customary loneliness. Around him the room's dimness swirled in shapes like angry screams. Nothing more specific showed itself, and she gave up, resuming her place on the bed.

Rough childhood, Josette thought. But there's a fair chance he knows that much himself. She wasn't going to get away with more than a couple of hundred for tonight, and no offering. Not even enough to break even. Not unless she at least got her client's pants off for him.

She let loose of the slumber. Her client stirred but didn't waken. Resistant, was he? Perhaps she'd been too sophisticated in her approach. She focused, made adjustments upward. Her sweat sharpened, breath hardened—not with delight, but with dirt-simple demand. A calculated grind brought her the contours of good news: through sleep's light draping Danny Woods had responded.

Suddenly his hands held her shoulders, twisting her clumsily, face down. The too-soft mattress shifted as he came to his knees, bore left and right as he stripped the denim off one leg, then the other. Then he was on her, kneading and nipping, urging her haunches higher. The sheath, she had to check the sheath, make sure she still had it in place. She freed one hand, felt the rolled rim, numb among her sensitive wrinkles, and braced herself once more, barely in time.

Without a word he thrust inside and worked away. Fierce, not fancy. Without a word, but soon not silently. Strange, muffled grunts, snuffles, snorts, and growls came from him as he rose and fell, rose and fell. The pace increased, as did the noise, and Josette risked another look into the closet mirror. Her heart jumped shut as she found and met them there, those yellow, glowing eyes. Held them, poised for flight or fight, those wild eyes of the beast. And stayed still, gazing as her blood slammed back through, opening its accustomed gates. Pulse pounding, she considered pretending not to notice the eyes, with pupils slit, not round, and the fur roughening her client's silhouette, already pretty vague within the mirror's frame. And without, his skin still seemed smooth and relatively hairless to her touch. It—he—obviously didn't expect he would be seen this way. After a short, puzzled pause he went back to his business. He made his offering and collapsed with her in a fairly graceful heap. From there he fell into another sleep, this time his own.

She lay and rested on her back awhile, feet up, knees held loosely to her chest so she wouldn't lose a drop. Throughout it all she'd felt no threat. Once she'd checked to find him unchanged outside the mirror, the fear, like dry ice, had evaporated, leaving no residue except an odd chill, and a lingering curiosity.

She glanced at the work candle. It still had a little more to burn. Should she tell her client about encountering the beast? She wasn't exactly sure of their relationship. Was the one the other's curse? Or totem animal? Was Danny Woods possessed, or just lost in a story he had no idea how to tell? A sudden tide of liquid wax swamped the candle's wick and snuffed it out, deciding her. She had done enough for one night.

She rose, picked up her toolkit, and felt her way into the bathroom, where she carefully removed the sheath. Singing softly. It had, after all, gone fairly well.

> Oh, when I was a lass at school,
> I looked up at the sky;
> And now among the woodlands cool
> Gathering sweet primroses, I . . .

She took her oversized tee and orange tights from her toolkit's bottom tray and sat down on the stool to pull them on. Leaving the door ajar for the light, she came back out to the bedroom. Her skirts were on the floor, still. She picked them up and smoothed them out, letting them hang over one arm.

"Josette—"

She turned. Danny Woods was awake. He had propped himself up on both his elbows. His hair swam over his bare shoulders, tangled currents running down the hollow of his back. "What?" she said.

"Nothing. Just—Josette."

She found the veil and rolled the skirts in it. Stuck the candle remains in a small brown paper bag, ready for disposal.

She paused at the door. What would it be like to stay with him, to hear his tale and tell him hers? A white man, but he hadn't committed any racist stupidities, at least not yet. The beast, though . . . and Viola. They might not like it, either one.

"Goodbye," he said, turning away.

"Okay," she said. She left.

The hallways were as murky as ever, night and day and night and day again. Outside some doors pairs of shoes stood, waiting to be polished, or stolen, or ignored. She called the elevator. It came quickly. They always did around four in the morning, convention or no.

Back in 1213 she drank a couple of glasses of tepid tap water, loaded the sheath's contents into a cryoflask and checked out Danny Woods' credit info. The card he'd given her had thirty-three hundred available. Low. Must be the one that he'd been traveling on. She took a third, but left the line open, undecided. Maybe it ought to be more . . . danger pay. But had she really been in danger?

She didn't know. She was tired, and so she shut it down.

It had been a long, long night, but she got out the candle fixings anyway: lavender and lotus and mugwort oil. Baby powder. Clover seed. A pinch of earth from Milham Park, in the town where she was born. And a blue ceramic bowl to mix them in.

She thought again about the house that afternoon. The wrong one, obviously. Holly had been right. Only, it was so long now since they had started looking. And Viola needed a home of her own so desperately.

Josette's eyes blurred. She blinked and shed quick, hot tears into the blue bowl.

Mix wet and dry ingredients with rapid strokes. One more thing, she thought, and lowered her head to the bowl. In, out, in again, she breathed the sweet, musty aroma. There.

She was in the middle of anointing the votive when a knock came at the door. She glanced at the radio. 5:45 A.M. She hadn't ordered any breakfast. She ignored the knock and kept working. It came again, a short while later. This time a white sheet of paper followed, sliding under her door.

The water on the altar looked a little cloudy. She changed it, then lit the new candle.

Her doll slept peacefully. Her small chest rose and fell steadily now, in the light of the low flame. It seemed a pity to disturb her, so

Josette packed as much as she could beforehand. Then it was almost seven. That would be a good nine hours.

She called a courier for the cryoflask, then picked up the phone again to order a cab for 8:30. The dispatcher put her on hold, to the tune of Sammy Davis Jr.'s "The Candy Man." While she waited, she gave in and read the note. Several times. It was short; all it said was "I love you." No signature. The handwriting belonged on a blueprint, even and precise.

The line clicked and the dispatcher was back. "To Metro," she told him. "My flight leaves at 10:30 A.M." She gave him the hotel's address, then asked, "Is Holly driving this morning?"

"I don't know. I can take a message for her, if you like."

On the bed, Viola stirred and pushed sleepily at the covers. "That's all right. Thanks."

"Thank you for calling Rite-Ride."

Josette went and sat on the bed. "Hey, squids, you ready to motivate?"

Viola smiled and stretched her short, fat arms. Josette loved to watch her wake up this way, with the candle going. The doll's face shone with joy.

But when she saw the suitcases, she sobered up a bit.

"Do we *have* to go already, Aunt Josette?"

"I'm afraid so, darling. There's no place for us here." She paused in buttoning up Viola's pink cardigan. The buttons were white and yellow daisy shapes. She twirled them around in her fingers while she spoke. "I think, maybe, yesterday was a good lesson."

"I was sad we couldn't get the house," Viola said.

"Yes, but . . . it wasn't right, it belonged to someone else. If we're going to start another temple, it has to really be our own. I think we're going to have to just make it. From scratch. From the ground up."

"Is that going to be a lot of work?"

"Probably." Josette pulled her blond mohair sweater over her head. It was big; it came down to her knees. "So we better get going. We've got enough saved up to buy some land that's really *beautiful*, maybe on a lake, even."

"Okay."

"What's the matter? You don't seem too enthusiastic, Viola."

"Auntie Josette, are you ever sorry you made me?"

She picked her doll up, cradled her in her wooly arms. "Oh, darling. *No.* Never. Before I had you, everything was horrible, just awful. I never got to smile or play, or anything. It was like I was dead, Viola. But now I'm alive, honey. 'Cause you're alive. And why would I be sorry about a thing like that?" She kissed Viola's long, black braids. "I love you, you silly squid!"

"And Bunny too?"

"And Bunny too. Now we better get you in the purse or we'll miss our ride to the airport." She got her doll to sit down in her handbag, with Bunny on her lap.

The stones were packed away. Only the votive and water remained. She snuffed the candle, emptied the water in the sink, stuck the still-warm votive in a wax bag in her coat pocket. Wheeled her bags out into the hall.

One last look around. Nothing left behind, she thought, and closed the door on 1213.

Down to the lobby. She was going to miss this floor.

The same clerk checked her out as in. Her eyes were red-rimmed now, from tears or smoke or lack of sleep, Josette couldn't tell. But her perky smile was identical. "Did you enjoy your stay?" she asked, trying to disguise her curiosity. The cryoflask gleamed cryptically on the beautiful, dark counter between them, waiting to be picked up.

"Oh, yes. Can you tell me, has the party in 1610 checked out yet?"

"Doesn't look like it. Want me to ring them?"

"Oh, no, it's too early. Just see that he gets this." The card was embossed, pearl on white. "Women Of The Doll," it read. "Tell us what you want." No address. Just a phone number, prefix 1-900. She was sure he would be using it. Any messages would be forwarded to her.

A car horn sounded outside. "Come again!" chirped the clerk as Josette hurried to the door. As she stooped to ease her luggage wheels over the threshold, she noticed a place where the marble floor was cracked. It looked loose. She pried up a small section and put it in her pocket. Bit by bit, she would build it, her own place. She and all the others. Piece by piece.

Something More

SHE WENT DOWN THE stairs. She wasn't going to fall like Mum had that time. The stairs were safe, broad, and tidily carpeted with a beige runner that hid the dirt. They were dull and familiar as the rest of the house where Allie had lived since she was a baby. The stairs were safe, and it was Mum's fault she'd come home from grammar school ten years ago to find her heaped on the landing.

The stairs turned a corner there. She stopped. No mirror had ever hung on this wall. Yet in the dusk she saw her reflection.

Allie came closer. The reflection stood still. No, it wasn't her, and anyway there was no frame around the figure standing so quietly.

No mirror frame or doorway, only the shadows of the corners melting away into a soft glow like candles backlighting the woman who was not Allie. Short and plump, but her skin was darker, even given the dimness surrounding them both, and her hair much crinklier, like a negro's. She wore different clothes too: a long dress, a flower print that looked flannel-ish, smocked from the shoulders to below her breasts. Her dark eyes widened as Allie approached. She opened her mouth and disappeared.

Allie's hand brushed the wall's olive paint with a dry sound like a whisper. Hadn't she seen the woman before? A dream, surely. Or another hallucination. What everyone else took drugs to get. She decided to draw her but say nothing about this latest episode to Mum. She continued down; her sketch pad was on the table in the entry hall with her nursing texts and Mike's letters from Australia.

Three steps from the bottom she caught at the baluster to save herself. Only a second, and things settled back down. She needed a drink. It never made things any worse. The times she remembered it seemed to have made them better.

In the sitting room, the mantel clock's round face read half six. Early yet. Lower and to the left, Mum's face looked up from her magazine with about as much expression. Allie wasn't like her. Never would be.

"Got a class?"

If Allie lied, Mum would find out. "No. 'M going to study." To study what mattered. The music.

"Take a wrap. It's not spring yet—"

The door cut off Mum's weather forecast. On the pavement Allie shrugged into the woolly cardigan she'd snatched from the hat stand, shifting her textbooks from arm to arm. April in Wimbledon meant sharp winds, low skies, and puddles to step around as she made her way to the bus stop. During the long ride she roughed out the lady from the landing in pencil, then did her again in pen, thinner. As she worked, Allie understood why she had thought her a mirror image, then believed she'd seen her somewhere before. The face was remarkably like her own—a little off from what she saw over the washstand each morning, but close enough. That must be it, she thought, and shut the book.

At the restaurant above Cousin's she lucked out. Bert and Justin were there eating supper. They chipped in and bought her a plate of goulash, pouring her drinks from their bottle of red wine. Justin winked at her and she only stared back. What a dish. Too bad he knew it.

But Bert was all right. He agreed to call her up for a couple of numbers so she could get in free. The club opened and they descended. Ginnie arrived along with some girls from Art School and ordered lagers all around. One of Ginnie's friends looked a little underage in her silver shift. Some of the others stank of weed despite an overlayer of patchouli. Ginnie too. Why they weren't such close pals as they used to be. Was she wanting to find again that way what Allie'd never totally gotten rid of?

Allie sang well. That good feeling came up within her, came over her and all around her and wrapped her inside itself. Music was something Mum never had. She did "Polly Vaughan" for the traddie crowd, and "It Ain't Me Babe," the only Dylan Bert ever covered. Carried along by the melodies she didn't have to worry what was up or down or left or right. Then she was let loose again. Her bit was over. Bert got on with his solo act while Justin obliged with a few gin and tonics.

She wound up going home to his flat with him, though there were plenty of better-looking birds than Allie within spitting distance. Life was a jumble of disjointed scenes by then: the cig they shared in the taxi and its driver cursing them as they dropped it, and the smell of the plastic seat cushion burning; the wet glint of the area steps down to Justin's door, which was how she realized it had started raining again; the red velvet of his Chesterfield soft under her cheek and his chest scratching her back as if it were covered in horsehair; his drunken wonder that he'd finally gotten her to fuck him: "Too tall fer ye, thas what I thought you thought, Allie, that you wunt nivver go with no bloke near twice yer height." And she laughed and fell in love. And then asleep.

#

In Allie's dream, the lady spoke. Her voice was sad, her words warnings and pleas for help. Allie needed to watch out for the wizard. Keep him at arm's length and keep track of him.

"He'll switch himself to a body in your time. We can do that trick, some of us. I could," the lady said. Allie knew her name, but not how to say it. "I could be in your place if I wanted."

They stood on a beach. Cows nosed through the washed-up kelp; wet sand threw back a wavering picture of their skinny brown legs and bulky bodies and the pewter sky above.

Allie tried to suss out what a wizard from the past would want with her. A nursing student. A singer.

The lady seemed to hear her thoughts. "It's me," she said. "He can hurt me through you."

If only Allie knew what he looked like she'd have an easier time spotting him.

"He'll probably have a beard and a mustache. He'll be powerful, even in your time. Special; a magician or something like that. Lots of women." She began to run both hands over her face as if wiping away weariness. "He looks like this—" she said, and Allie awoke in Justin's arms.

#

Justin had a mustache and a beard, and as many women as he ever wanted. A moment more Allie let her eyes linger on the tumbling of his red-brown hair, on his noble jaw even longer now, relaxed in sleep. But what did he see in her? Likeness to the lady?

Slipping from his side and picking her way across the flat's cluttered floor, she dressed at hazard and escaped. Outside it was barely morning, clouds like wadded chips papers scudding low. Kicking wet rubbish from her path she slouched off to Cambridge Circus to find a cab home, already regretting her decision to ditch him.

Her dreams and hallucinations had slowed down during secondary school, then picked up again when she started her internship at Brompton Hospital. It maybe had something to do with being near so many people about to die.

Possibly she shouldn't pay any attention to them. She was nothing like Mum.

Allie ran into Justin again a week later. He seemed a bit puzzled but friendly enough; no indication he wanted to pick up where they'd left off, and she convinced herself he simply didn't remember. Which hurt, of course, but also made her feel less a fool.

She locked love away with her other secrets.

"Are you happy, now?" she wanted to ask the lady, but she was absent from Allie's apparitions for a while, months and months. Over a year. Until the audition.

Allie had been singing all along, alone and with a skifflish band, getting better and better. Last quarter she'd quit school for it. Going for her dream now, not Mum's safe bet: off with the white Oxfords and on soon enough with paisley shawls from Carnaby Street boutiques.

Allie was on her way to Top of the Pops; none of these men had ever heard her, though. What a motley lot, she thought, watching them warm up in the pub they'd commandeered for the afternoon. Longhairs in denim and jerseys, not a wizard among them.

They could play, particularly the lead guitarist, a gawky, camel-faced lad called Henry. She gave them "The Shooting of His Dear," her strongest folk number, then followed that with her own "Just Before the Dawn." Let her voice carry her beyond the four walls on its broad currents, brushing up ripples of sound with the turn of her tongue, only ruffling the surface so they could feel how deep it went, sweeping quietly along till the climax and crashing down in great waves over the stones of the last words to swirl in the still pool of the end.

The bassist looked at the drummer. "Quite." They all grinned.

Not that night but the next, the lady reappeared. In the intervening year she had grown no older. She wore the same dress. The sea shone in the distance like mercury. They met on the balcony of a white marble building, a temple of some sort, Allie thought. The lady's pleas were more urgent than ever, but impossible to get the sense of. Finally she summoned another person, a brown-skinned man who left and quickly returned with a pad and a crayon set.

Have you found him yet? wrote the lady. She sat on a bench and patted a place for Allie beside her.

I think so, Allie wrote.

Has he tried to kill you?

Frightened, Allie shook her head. That was why she was supposed to be on guard? She wished the lady had explained better. Didn't you say he was after you, not me? she scrawled. She looked around. Against white clouds, blue birds with wingspans like a gull's soared. This was a dream, right? She could wake up, like last time—

Danger, the lady wrote hastily. Don't go yet. He can hurt me through you. Are you sure you know who it is? You're getting closer to the— The lady balled her fists and made a frustrated face. —the thing that might happen.

Justin? Or another bearded man with heaps of lovers? Can you draw him? Allie asked, and the lady sketched out a colored man, shoulders up, hair a tangle of leafless twigs, eyes squinting with laughing malevolence. An expression she'd never seen on easygoing Justin.

Her love.

No, that's not him, she managed to write, blinking, which only made the tears spill onto her cheeks.

The lady grabbed the pad back and wrote furiously, her crayon strokes wide with pressure. Find him first! Before he finds you! Otherwise it is all over.

What was over? Why?

He wants to come back there. Escape. And fight me through how he messes up the lines you make. It will be easy unless I can use your— The lady drew an upside-down triangle with a vertical line running from apex to base only to scribble it out and continue writing. —body.

Use her body? What was the difference between that and death? Allie regarded the lady skeptically. A negro, no matter how similar some of their features. What reason did Allie have to help her? To believe her? If not for the lady's warning, Allie and Justin would be together. Without much effort, a kind of half twist of her head, she left.

Waking slowly, face still wet with tears, Allie couldn't stomach how naive she'd once been. Only eighteen, and such a child. Why had she ever even trusted the lady? She looked a lot like Allie—that meant nothing. Coincidence, nothing more.

Now she was nineteen, almost twenty; a shot or two at bedtime chased the visions away. Allie focused on her career. Rehearsal ate up big blocks of time. The recording sessions. Then gigs in cellars around town, new nightspots, to support the album. Afterwards she'd go out drinking with the band and Justin would show up, often with his new wife.

They bought a van and hit the road. Clubs were starting up outside London too. They drove back home when they were done, most of the time. Ginnie tagged along; there was plenty of room, even with their equipment, and she brought the smoke. Allie kept the windows cranked down as much as possible. Owners gave them knowing looks anyway as they piled out reeking and snickering. Not that plenty of them didn't take their fair share of drugs themselves.

Allie dug her knuckles in her back and arched. Cool shadows covered the dark brick walls on either side of the alley. This place had its own sound system, but they'd still have to haul their instruments up. For once they were playing aboveground. Easier to load downhill at the end of the night.

Geordie and Nick emerged from the covered stairway laughing at some joke she hadn't heard. Allie acted like she was about to pick up Henry's guitar case. "Here!" Nick handed her a snare. "He'll want his girl to take that up if he don't."

His girl? Allie would have expected Ginnie to go after somebody better looking. But when they passed each other in the club's doorway Ginnie had Henry by the hand, and she was wearing that look, sleek and alert, eyes blazing, cheeks full of blood, scent high and warm. More power to her.

Allie made another three trips, for a crash cymbal, her purse, and her own guitar, not that she used it onstage anymore with the band. But she wasn't going to leave it lying about in the open after making Mum buy it with money meant for Mike.

The floor creaked. Lacquer smell crept up from the furniture shop below. No dressing room to speak of; an hour before the show they crowded into the office of the owner, a nervous chap in a pearl-snapped shirt who refused to sit in his own chair. Geordie and Iain did a good job soothing him. Nick made sticks of his fingers and worked over the waste can and the sides of the desk, its drawers and handles . . . he hated waiting as much as she did.

At last there were enough tables full when the owner peeked round the edge of his office door. Time to take the stage. Allie stoppered up the Drambuie bottle.

Outside the spotlight, no one besides the band. Inside it, her and her voice. She rocked and cradled the sound as it came out. Whispered feather breaths. Cried notes hard as churchstones.

Then it was over again.

She and Iain helped Nick pack his gear while Geordie settled up. Henry and Ginnie had disappeared. Naturally. Supposedly off to fetch curries for the lot of them. Allie wasn't hungry; a good thing considering the weight she'd put on lately.

She gave Nick the eye. Something special about him: the time he kept, the beat he found. His wild hair and hollow-faced intensity. Nothing meant for her there, though. He was looking straight at her, but he didn't seem to notice what he saw.

Iain? He smiled back at her as she tied down the top of the big bass case. She headed casually over to the table where he was stashing tools in a kit. Stood there in stupid silence till he shut the toolkit and picked it up and walked away.

So she was fat. So what? She was getting more and more famous. The band stayed on the circuit and she met other musicians, also famous, from around the world. Allie slept with some, fucked a few more.

One threw a scare into her despite her hard-won cynicism, his skin and hair so similar to the lady's portrait. And the Fu Manchu mustache and goatee, and the hordes of groupies eager to make it with a Black, and the way his first album almost edged the Beatles out of the top spot. It took a full tumbler of gin before she gathered the courage to show up at his hotel. A waste. In the morning she recalled nothing except the lady shaking her disembodied head in a darkened window on the fourteenth floor, a reflection of someone not there. Never there.

It was Bert who informed her of Justin and Connie's separation. They were all three at the same table in a nameless pub. Allie had no idea how she'd gotten there, but she knew how she left. She put her hand over Justin's as it lay on the greasy tabletop and he let it rest there a moment, then turned his palm up to mesh his fingers with hers and lifted it and she floated off in his tow, following him out the door, under the sparkling stars, and gently drifted to the ground on the pavement in front of his latest digs.

He gave her hand a squeeze and dropped it, charmingly awkward as he fished out his keys and smiled and asked, "Will ye stay a while longer this time?"

#

She knew she was happy. He was too, but she was the one who knew. And you couldn't call it cheating, what he did, when they made up the rules as they went.

The lady kept trying to intrude. Her face appeared in bottle sides, on bath water—spreading out ring-wise under the spigot, or material-izing from mounds of suds like cloud-pictures when Allie switched to foaming crystals. Her voice echoed in the background of demo tapes. "Listen, listen," she sang, for nobody but Allie to hear.

Then the ill-fated day. Allie woke up crying and couldn't tell anyone why. She didn't know. Her happiness had suddenly vanished, like the glitter on a wave-cap when the sun goes. The band were on tour, but when it came time to climb in the van she couldn't do it. She called Justin and he agreed to meet her at the hotel and bring her on to the next stop separately.

They waited at the service entrance to the pub where the band had been booked for that night. No sign of the others, and no equipment or instrument cases to indicate they'd already been and gone looking for cheaper alcohol. At last the manager came toward them, swaggering and stooping at the same time, studying the boards under his pointy-toed boots. He'd been too busy for questions when they came in, but now he stood silent a moment before speaking.

"Bit of an accident," he said. "'Course I know it ain't in the contract, but if you could help us out solo, maybe your young man here might accompany you—"

"Accident? What sort of accident would ye be talkin' about?" Justin asked. His long left arm went around Allie's shoulder. She sank against his side, shivering in the March sun.

The van had overturned. The drummer, the manager said. Nick. And Ginnie. Dead.

Justin drove her to see the survivors, Iain with both legs broken, the others pretty cut up but basically all right, physically.

Henry had fallen asleep at the wheel. Henry had caused the wreck. Ginnie had become his bird. Barely a scratch on him.

He lay in a hospital bed, stoned on prescription drugs. Heavy sedation to keep the hysterics at bay. Allie read the doses on his chart. It would be a long while till he came to.

She sat by him and held his spider-fingered hand anyway. Perhaps he'd be able to feel it in his unconscious state. Tears slid down her cheeks continually, but that wasn't a problem, really. Plenty of tissue boxes in a hospital. She sent Justin for carry-out, not terribly surprised when he stayed away past closing. Ginnie had been one of his too.

Allie made shameless use of her old Brompton credentials, and the night nurse overlooked her presence after visiting hours.

Later, she snapped awake in the chair to find Henry staring at her. Or someone. Henry's face above Henry's body, and his arm still attached to the hand that she still held. But in the eyes, another. A dream, she thought, and then Henry's mouth opened and that other spoke. A foreign tongue.

"Pardon?" She wanted to look away. Didn't manage to.

"Huh," said the voice in Henry's mouth. "Gonna gotta. Power uppin." English now. Sort of. Drool spun a silver thread down his chin. Allie thrust his hand back on the bed and let go. Or tried to. Their palms clung together like doomed lovers.

"Yessss. Ya see?"

Allie did. Henry's eyes—whatever looked through them—the exact same expression as the lady's drawing—

She strained to turn her head, to snatch back her hand.

The wizard snickered. "Wuss wrong?" He sounded no more than slightly buzzed now. The grip on her hand tightened. His other arm swung up stiffly and hovered above the tray next to the bed, knocking over a water glass to shatter on the lino. Thin, strong fingers wadded the fabric of her bodice into a knot and pulled her closer, closer into his embrace. Unavoidable his chapped lips, hollow laughter, writhing tongue something white on it, pushing pills bitter between her teeth salt with blood her own—

"Here, you! None of that!" The night nurse, pulling her free, slammed her back in her seat. Allie coughed and retched and the pills came up. She caught them in her fist, slimy with spit. The nurse never noticed, fussing over Henry, summoning help. His eyes were shut. Shamming it?

"Best you leave, Miss," the night nurse said over her shoulder as more staff came in, her tone stern and fearful at the same time. Well, it was her watch, and if it came out she'd let Allie stay . . .

Picking up her purse, Allie stumbled out of the room, down the hall to the elevator. On the street, unfriendly lamps lit intersections glistening with wet. She had no idea which way their hotel was, where Justin had got to.

Right before the road curved a golden light spilled from an opening door which quickly shut to extinguish it. When she got there it was what she'd pictured, a pub. Not the one where they had been going to play, but another, older, better, full of strangers.

After a couple of good drinks she felt more like herself. She remembered the hotel's name and found a payphone and left Justin a message. Another couple and she was ready at last to cry, so she excused herself to the well-meaning poofter on her right, went to the Ladies' and locked the door.

"Oh, Ginnie! Oh, Nick!" Ginnie had been Allie's mate since primary, when she'd fancied Allie's brother Mike. She sat on the wooden toilet seat and howled her grief to the muddy green walls till someone knocked on the door. She couldn't stop. But she slowed down enough to tell them bugger off, and shortly they did.

No privacy in a public convenience. Allie slopped water on her face from the warm trickle the sink supplied. Avoiding the mirror out of habit. The thin, damp roll of toweling scraped comfortingly against her skin. Her eyes still leaked a bit, and snuffles and sobs punctuated her breathing.

Another knock, loud and hard. His. Allie opened the door and there he was, waiting to take her home. Or what passed for it on tour.

Justin steered one-handed, hugging her to him in the dark. The lady ghosted along next to them, a faint reflection in the window. When they got to the room, they made fierce love, tears falling on her face, then his, as they changed position. Her first sleep was dreamless, but when Allie roused drowsily for a midnight pee, the lady showed up in the mirror. Her mouth moved. No sound came out of it.

Allie went back to bed expectantly and wound up by the sea again. She and the lady sat in bent willow chairs on the ledge of a cliff.

"You're becoming quite handy at this, aren't you?" the lady asked. She had an animal on her lap, something like a dog, something like a miniature giraffe.

Allie shrugged.

"Are you able to talk now?"

"I—yes," Allie said, surprised.

"Good. And why are we dreaming to each other again?"

"'Why?' It's—So you can warn me, or—"

The lady shook her head, then glanced aside, stroking her strange pet's head. "Something has happened. The dreams are all about the time getting stronger. What has—"

"He killed them! My friends—"

"The wizard?"

"Oh, god, they're gone . . ." Allie felt sorrow fill her throat like laryngitis. It was real even here, in this dream—

"Tell me!"

Allie dragged her words out through the pain. "It looked like an accident. Henry flipped the van, but it wasn't him, it was him, I think—but Henry's white and he doesn't have a beard, and girls don't usually go—" She stopped, then started again and told the story right.

"Yes," the lady said. "It was our enemy. In a body so unlike his own—I would not believe it. But you are still alive." She stood, cradling the animal in her arms, and walked a few steps along the ledge. Allie saw the temple far behind her. Tall men in grey walking toward them from it.

"What should I do?" Allie asked.

"He may not stay. Only a little while he could be in this body till he finds another better. It is bad, the way he takes them."

"Okay. Then—"

"Nothing. Hide from him and he will find you. Only watch and wait. You can do nothing more.

"Unless you let me in." She turned to stare at Allie.

Oh, no. "Like the wizard in Henry."

"Different—I am no evil! Here they come!" The lady pointed at the tall negroes approaching. She looked all around as if hunting for a safe place. Afraid of them? Weren't they her servants? "Take me now, please! No! Don't—"

But Allie was already awake. No one would use her.

#

As soon as he got out, Iain insisted on a rehearsal. Before that they were all avoiding each other. Allie's behavior must have seemed ordinary enough under the circumstances.

She made a halfhearted attempt to argue herself out of belief. Dreams were all in your head. Her hallucinations were nothing more. Then she found the pills in the dress pocket where she'd shoved them when leaving the wizard's bedside.

So.

The wizard existed. Who knew about the lady? No sign of her anyway since that night. But the wizard. If he wasn't evil, he was as nasty a piece of work as Allie wanted to come up against.

She intended to miss that first rehearsal, and maybe every one after. She sat curled up in the window seat of the flat she and Justin shared—had shared—with Ginnie, a bottle beside her, and watched unbelieving as Iain's Cortina pulled up to the kerb and Henry—or the thing using him—came out of the driver's side. The passenger door opened too, a crutch shoving it wide as Henry-or-whoever caught it by the handle. Iain stood, both casts off but still a bit wobbly on his pins, and they looked up at her window. Allie jerked back, but of course it was too late.

"Oi! You making me come up all them bloody steps, then?"

She hid in the bath, but Justin picked that moment to return from wherever he'd spent the night and they trailed in behind. "Only we've got a new drummer to try out today, see, and it don't matter if she's a bit sloshed, but it'd help if she could be there—" Iain groused.

"Not to worry—Allie!"

The window was too small to climb out of. Her stomach clutched and she knelt in front of the toilet bowl waiting to be sick—surely then they'd leave her alone? The lady's face looked up at her, a double exposure over her own. "Not letting you use me. Not on your life," Allie whispered to the cool, still water. The door rattled in its frame against the flimsy lock.

An echo off the porcelain softly repeated her words: "your life . . . life . . ."

The salt taste rushed into her mouth and a spasm like anger rose through her, acid vomit spewing out. Crying, she heaved again, and again, then collapsed on the floor, muscles sore. She hated this. Fucking cognac.

Forced herself back up to flush. Spatters on the bowl's rim, such a mess, what would Mum say? Allie ravaged the roll of its paper and swabbed off her mouth and the rest. Rinsed and mopped again. Justin called to her that they'd left and she came out and they were still there. Out of the actual flat and waiting on the stairs, so it wasn't a lie, really. One look at her and they did go.

Had that been Henry? Truly Henry? To all appearances; but Allie wasn't sure she could trust her own judgment.

As usual, Justin showed his regret through giving her loads of attention, hugs and kisses that this time broke her down in his arms. Weeping, she tried to say what was wrong and only managed to make him think she was pregnant. He rocked her back and forth in the short passageway, bent over her like a sheltering tree, nuzzling her hair.

"Shush, shush, we're getting married I promise, sweetie, darlin, how long? You were gonna keep it a secret? Oh, Allie . . ."

He seemed so happy. Would marriage mean more time with him, attention like this every day? She hated to tell him no, it was all a silly mistake. Because she was pretty sure she wasn't pregnant—nursing school lessons. And it wasn't the sort of thing she'd let happen: invasion, someone else inside. But it did give her the idea that maybe. Later. When she could make herself surrender.

So she waited a couple of weeks to tell him. To give herself a taste of what it would be like.

Suddenly solicitous, Justin accompanied Allie to her first few rehearsals. No sign of any wizard in Henry, who seemed his old self. Not quite the same, but then nobody was. One thing: he'd begun writing songs.

The new drummer, Ned, caught on quick. Quite professional. "Slow march," Henry told him, played his latest tune once, and Ned laid the rhythm down like that.

The words were about Nick and Ginnie. Allie learned them and sang lead on the verses, harmony with Henry on the chorus. Hardly flinched when he bent to share the mike with her.

Maybe the wizard was gone, had left like the lady said he might. But what went away could come back.

Iain's great-aunt had a house in Hampshire she let. He wanted them all there for the summer to write new material and record their next album. And put the accident behind them. Justin drove Allie, as she couldn't yet bring herself to ride anywhere with the others. He was meant to stay too, but at a restaurant on the way she finally told him there was no child.

"No?" He glanced down at the table where they sat, a charming spot under bee-buzzing vines in flower, good local ale glowing brownly in glass-bottomed mugs. Then looked up, his face puzzled. "Weren't there ever?"

Her love. How could she hurt him? "No. I only—I thought, but—" She wouldn't, wouldn't make it any worse. "I knew, but you seemed so glad I—"

"How long?" Horrible echo of his question when he asked her in the flat, when she let him think she was. "When did you—did you always? You knew?"

Numb, she nodded.

He got up, not letting their eyes meet. "Right. Let's go then." And headed for the carpark. She dawdled, drank her beer, his too before she joined him in the green Triumph where he waited, grimly patient. Silent.

He said not a word the rest of the trip. Allie tried to start a fight. Next morning she woke with the feeling she'd succeeded at last after they arrived at Iain's aunt's. Shouts and slamming doors. But what had it been about? Something trivial. Something slight. She could fix it quite easily, if only she could find him.

He'd left the house. No one would take her back to London, not till the weekend.

There was a train. She phoned the flat so he'd come to meet it. No reply.

No reply. No reply. And no reply.

Well fuck-all use going home if he hadn't.

Allie put little faith in the lock on her bedroom door. It looked merely decorative, a polite vestige of the days when Iain's aunt hosted parties of visitors for a fortnight or more. What would keep out a wizard, anyway? Did you have to invite them in, like a vampire? She had depended on Justin for protection, planned on his presence. How would she survive?

She would.

After that first night she shoved a chairback under the door handle. Henry wouldn't be able to open it without waking her, and whatever the wizard's power, it had to be contained in Henry's body.

The lady would be easy to avoid, Allie thought. Stay away from reflective surfaces. Then encountered her as she had at the beginning, on a stair landing. Heading up to her room from a session with the band, working on another of Henry's new songs, this one about a woman turned into a swan and accidentally killed by her lover, and there, a flight of steps going off the other direction than the one they always took before. The real steps were dimmed out somehow; the false set shone with a flickering yellow light, and on the topmost stood her Black twin.

Beckoning. Allie found herself moving towards the false flight of stairs. Why? The lady smiled apologetically as Allie put her foot on the lowest bright step. Then the next. The sounds of the country house cut off, and a fresh wind twisted a lock of hair loose and brushed it against her face. They were outdoors, the yellow flickers of sunlight fallen through leaves fluttering overhead.

The lady collapsed forward, and Allie caught her. She looked for somewhere to lay her. The steps were white marble now, leading down not to the landing in Iain's aunt's house but to a terrace or walk covered with black and purple tatters, dead leaves. A backless bench waited obligingly. She struggled over to it and lowered the lady to sprawl there unconscious. She lifted her feet up onto it too. They were bare and calloused.

Someone stood behind her. It was one of the tall Blacks. Where had he sprung from? He bent over the lady, his dark face concerned. "She just fell," Allie said. "All I did was keep her from hitting the ground." He appeared not to hear her. After touching the lady's hands, somewhat hesitantly, then grasping her chin and waggling her head back and forth, he lifted her off the bench and walked away.

Allie, frightened, followed. The negro climbed the steps. They ended, and another terrace stretched ahead. How was she going to get back? The lady was her only connection. Allie had to almost run to stay up. Past trees with black and red and purple foliage, the wind blowing sharper here. They must be by the shore or up above it; she glimpsed the sea to her left through the trees, grey and wrinkled with waves. A long, low building rose on her right. She recognized the temple as it grew larger, and then they entered it. Animals lounged out of their way, things like zebras but orange and maroon, with markings like letters she ought to be able to read.

The Black turned into an open doorway and deposited the lady on a bed covered in silver fur. The lady made a sound, a light whining with her mouth shut. So she was alive. Fainted. When she woke, she'd want to sick. Allie looked around for something to catch it in. The Black went away. A table, empty. Rugs on the walls, tapestries, like in a medieval castle. A chest of drawers, and a sort of alcove to one side with another, longer hanging blocking it off. Allie got up to investigate those, but then saw a bowl on the window sill. That would do. She set it on the floor near the bed's head.

The lady's skin was too dark to tell whether her circulation was normal by looking at her face. Allie peeled back one eyelid, then the other, watching the pupils dilate. She reached for the lady's wrist. Her pulse checked out weak but steady, no skipping, and neither fast nor slow.

Without proper drugs, there was nothing more she could do for her. Allie went back to the window, which overlooked the cliff and the sea. A sheer drop of at least three stories to the ground. The alcove was a closet, clothes hanging from hooks set in its walls. She recognized the dress the lady had worn on the stair landing at Wimbledon.

She stuck her head out the arched opening they'd entered the room by. No grey-clad negroes in sight; then one appeared, and others behind him, far off up the corridor between white marble columns. As if by magic—well, what else was all this?

A soft sound from the bed and Allie got the bowl in position just in time. The lady's vomitus was scanty and mustard-colored. Nothing to wipe off her mouth with. The lady lay back on the furs again and used her own sleeve, making a face and squeezing her eyes shut. "It worked," she whispered, her voice clotted. "I am the mightier poet. You're here." She coughed and lifted herself on her elbows and Allie got the bowl ready again, but the lady gestured it away.

"Wasn't I here before, then?" Allie asked. "Those dreams—"

"Were dreams."

This wasn't? No, of course, she'd known that. One minute climbing up to her room to fetch her guitar, the next—Where?

The three tall Blacks she'd seen outside the room came in. About to ask for an explanation, Allie thought better. They ignored her, though. One of them gave the lady a silver cup, something smelly and dark in it. Afterwards, she was sure they hadn't said a single word, but at the time they seemed to talk among themselves and to the lady. Grave expressions, meaningful looks exchanged, and a smoothness coordinating their movements with each other; when she thought back, it was these things that must have made that wrong impression on her. Two of them departed in silent unison.

The third, a dappled feather stuck in his short-clipped hair, folded himself to sit below the bed's foot. Allie tried to get his attention. "Hullo?" No good. She waved her hand in front of his face and he blinked.

"He can see you," the lady said from the furs where she lay. "However, he doesn't believe you matter. It would be a waste of energy to acknowledge your existence."

"But—"

"Yes, yes, you are real, you are here, I have brought you, so let's talk as I wanted to before."

"You brought me here?"

"For a little. Now listen—"

"You can send me back, then."

"Listen! When I say I can use your body, it's not like what you imagine and I kill you. No. I'm in you—your breath, your hands and feet, I feel your feelings, but I'm not your brain! I am not the boss. I only ride, a passenger. You fly, you. You're the pilot. As I would be if you used me the same."

Allie sat on the cold stone floor, shoving the bowl aside. "What do you mean?" She remembered the hospital. "The wizard—"

"He! Yes, you saw what he can do. How—" The lady shuddered. "Like eating food alive. I couldn't! Horrible!"

The lady leaned over the edge of her bed and grabbed Allie's shoulder. "And when he's done, and that one has no more use, he will move on to others. If he hasn't already. You must help me stop him!"

Allie turned her head to look at the Black man, who would not look back. Up to the window, anywhere but the lady's eyes.

Part of her wanted to do it. To show she wasn't afraid. That skin color wasn't important.

"All right, then. If you tell me you would do it too." The other part couldn't believe what she'd just said. "Only if you send me home now!" she added quickly.

"Yes! I chose right to make myself on you of all my family. And you have my promise I will take you in if it comes to a reverse." The lady shoved herself up from the bed. She fell right back onto it. "Still so weak. Then you take it out of the drawer for me," she said, pointing at the chest. "Please." An afterthought, but Allie went anyway.

"This?" she asked. A pad of sketching paper similar to the one the man had brought before, when they sat on the balcony. The lady nodded. Loose pastels and chalks lay scattered on and around it, and Allie gathered those up as well.

The Black man had stuffed pillows and furs behind the lady, propping her up at an angle. She took the pad from Allie and frowned, selecting a hexagonal purple column and a wine-red stub from the colors Allie offered her. She was left-handed. The design she started looked like lace.

"Can I ask you something?"

The lady stopped, keeping the tip of her pastel against the page, unmoving. "There's no time."

Questions boiled up in Allie and whirled around her head. She could almost see them multiply. "Well, but what's so awful about this bloody wizard, then? What's he up to—besides killing off all my friends and frightening me, but why would you care? And if you do—"

Allie paused to allow the lady to answer. "I care because I am good. And you are my model. So I save you." That was it. Allie waited longer, but she stayed silent, lips folded shut as if suppressing comment. Her lips so like Allie's own, and why? In a moment the lady's hand began twitching across the paper again, leaving a twisty labyrinth behind. The Black watched with interest. Another came through the arch to join him. And where were the white people?

"If you do care and you can bring me here, why not journey forward yourself to my time in your own body and—"

"'Forward'?" The lady picked up the red chalk in her right hand and drew with it at the same time as her left, intricate lines that almost but never quite crossed.

So complicated seeming. The lines crept together, pulled apart, together again, and ran in parallel. Allie had been talking. Asking something. What was it? She remembered and went on. "And I'll help you too, in my body, when we get there—"

"You think you came here from the future. But have you ever heard of such a place as this in history?" Both hands hung unmoving over the page. The lady stared fiercely at her lacework. "I am about to begin the last and most difficult part. Your time is in the past. Don't interrupt me anymore, or we won't make it all the way back."

In the past. This was the future. The plants and animals even were strange: the blue gulls, the dark-leaved trees. How far had she come?

She struggled to ask despite the lady's warning, but the red and purple lines went on too long. Years? Centuries? How far?

#

"Not more than a couple steps. At most."

"Who found her?"

Allie ached. She slit her eyes open. A blur of bluegreen like mildew washed over her senses. Close them, she thought practically, and did. She had hit her head somehow, probably fallen again. Bad one this time.

"Young Geordie. I sent him to phone her mum. And Justin."

So they had known where he was all along. Someone had. "Sod off," she wheezed, and tried to roll on her side. Something soft prevented her.

"You coming round then?"

"No." Slowly she raised her lids again the least little bit. A bolster of nauseous hue. Eyes right. Focus. Half the band stood around her bed, Iain and Ned and Dick the fiddler. Where was Nick? Oh.

Dead. Oh.

Funny how she'd known who Ned was but forgot the accident.

Right at that moment she remembered the lady too and everything that had happened or would happen up then. The future. And that she, Allie, had agreed to—to what? Let herself be possessed? By a Black?

She couldn't tell if she felt any different. Though hadn't she ought to be puking? Thank god not.

The band took it in turns to watch her through the night. She wouldn't let them drive her to the emergency clinic, fending off their concern with the authority of her old nursing internship, dribs and drabs of facts from her textbooks, anything to prevent a doctor prescribing the same seizure meds Mum got.

Henry-or-whoever showed up for his shift at three. He gave her shoulder a shake to wake her as the others had, but she wasn't sleeping.

"What's your name?" he asked, the question she'd told them to use to check her coherency.

"Mary Queen of Scots," Allie replied unhesitatingly. She pretended to shut her eyes. He laughed. It was Henry's laugh.

Her turn. "Who are you?"

He took so long to answer she thought he might not.

"A prisoner freed." He reached for the lamp on the bedside table, pulled it nearer. Nothing frightening in his face, his expression. His eyes seemed oddly knowing. "I mean your friends no harm. Nor you."

"You killed Nick and Ginnie."

"Not because I tried to." He hung his head; for shame of doing wrong? "You only fell a few feet. What if you'd been at the wheel when she showed herself that first time?"

Which was a lie, or something like it, Allie knew. But she couldn't say how, except he wasn't as innocent as he claimed. Trying to shove those sedatives down her throat at the hospital.

"Where's Henry?" She had to piss like a race horse. She tossed the covers aside and only then noticed she'd nothing on but her shirt and knickers.

"He's here still."

The wizard got out of her way and she stood up. "Well, let me talk to him. What's your name?"

He looked embarrassed, maybe by what she wasn't wearing. "It isn't a word," he said.

She made it to the toilet on her own, then needed a bit of help back to bed. Sliding between the cool sheets, she wanted badly to shut her eyes. But when she did a light built up behind them, a gold humming inside her. She opened them; it was less noticeable then.

"Where's Henry?" she repeated.

"Allie." That sounded more like him somehow. "Not to worry. 'M all right."

Allie kept him—or them—talking till half five. Mostly she heard from the wizard, who had lots to say compared to Henry, about how wizards and poets and rulers were all the same thing in the future and spent their lives in temples that were jails almost, guarded day and night. Not because of any danger; just to stop them leaving, by the sound of it.

"I got away," the wizard bragged. "My—the one to me like you are to the lady—comes years later, but I'm that good I could leave for now, for this time before him."

She lay on her back listening to him, watching the faint light pulse between her and the ceiling. The lady. Who was not forcing her to do stuff she didn't want to do.

Allie kept asking questions and the wizard kept answering them. Should she trust him? Or the lady, who'd refused to tell her anything? Her head ached.

What had the lady said about making herself "on" Allie? According to the wizard they were related somehow. By blood? She was the lady's ancestor? Maybe. Yes. And something more. An emulation he called it. And the lady had told Allie, "He can hurt me through you." So, Allie reasoned, if she, Allie, died the lady might never be born, and the wizard, who had ruled another land, or written another kind of poetry, or however it went, would win.

But the wizard would rather stay back here. Back now. In this time. "More fun than all that fighting," he said, half-smiling the way Henry did. "On my best behavior; that's a promise." So was the lady wrong about what he wanted?

The light stirred round and round, like cream in tea. Imagine what Mum would have to say about a Black for a granddaughter, great-granddaughter, great-great-great . . .

Loud as a cracker in the early morning silence the bedroom door opened, unsticking from its frame. "Here, I brought you a lemonade." It was Iain. The tumbler, blessedly cool, fit perfectly in the curve of her hand. Along its transparent sides streams of bubbles quivered, rising to prick her nose. Suddenly parched, she downed it in one quick gulp.

The wizard left. Under Iain's quiet gaze, clutching his hand, Allie slept three more hours. No dreams. When she woke she felt so much better she slipped out on her own for a walk, ending on the banks of a pond. She kicked away the sheep droppings and lay on her stomach in the shade of a young tree with nice, normal green leaves, looking down at the still water.

All she saw was her own face until a sleek rat dove from a shadowy hole to paddle to the pond's center. The surface rippled and the edges of her reflection grew shockingly bright, rainbows of color shooting out as if her head hid the sun. When the water settled the effect vanished. Allie stretched out one hand and stirred it to see if she could cause it to happen again. Delicious; a cool gladness suffused her fingers, and the lovely scents of mud and weeds wafted up, newly released to the spring air.

The pond was of course in a slight valley. She heard Justin's voice calling her. Then his head appeared. He didn't see her yet. She sat up.

He spotted her and grinned, though she could tell he was trying to frown. He ran down the slope and arrived not a bit out of breath. "Well, ye look in fine feather, Allie." He rubbed a broad palm along her back as he sat beside her. "Despite reports to the contrary."

"I—"

"Shush, now. Quiet. All forgiven." He tutted at her, shook an admonishing finger; "I know ye doan't mean a quarter a the things ye say when ye're droonk like that." He rose to his knees and gathered her in his arms, pulled her up against him and she felt her cunt throb like a second heart. He leaned to kiss her throat and soon they lay half-naked together on the fresh-bruised grass.

"I was thinkin."

Allie laughed. "When?"

Justin smiled. "Afore I come here, natch. About a new group. You and me in it."

He slapped lazily at her arse. "Ant," he said. "Time to get dressed."

They talked more. It was a marvelous idea; it would keep her out of the wizard's reach. And make her stop remembering Nick and Ginnie so much, which was why Justin had suggested it, she was sure. In the studio Iain had set up in his aunt's billiards room, Allie was all business. They laid the album's tracks so quickly Iain couldn't possibly object when she left. Well, he could have. Justin must have put a stop to that.

He took such care of her. And said never a word about them having a baby.

So many songs; they came easily these days, without trying. A few critics complained about her "needlessly obscure" lyrics. She wanted to cry, the first review like that she read, to tell them if the meaning was known, the magic was lost. All the visions she had never shared, even with Ginnie, she poured into her music now: walking up the tower's spiral stairs, wide windows in the stone walls and at every one another scene, all perspective forfeit as through the first, far below on the grass pale cobblers nailed together enormous boots, and through the next, tiny men in cockleshell hats sailed egg-cups over seas filled with drowning sailors

. . . and a flight of larks lifted a veil of glittering mist from the land and it melted apart in the sky into stars

. . . and the lady would be with her always.

That was where and when Allie had seen her before. Back when she was a lass at school. Now she only felt her, or rather, felt the lady feeling. She waited in vain for some summons to battle. None came.

#

Allie rode the bus to the studio, a line she never took. She'd used a clinic in a neighborhood full of West Indians; she felt more comfortable around them these days, since she was part-Black herself with the lady inside. Sort of. In a way.

The test was positive. She had known it would be this time, as she'd known not to bother with it before, when she lied.

Nothing bad had happened when she let the lady inside her. Having a baby would be all right. It would be worth it. And it wouldn't make her anything like Mum.

She stepped carefully down to the kerb, clinging to the bus door's polished steel handle. So how to tell him now it was true? At least the doctor's office would back her up.

Past the new receptionist, Tracy, that was her name, then the long climb up the stairs that crunched beneath her sandals like fresh snow. Hot, not cold, though, and the temperature rising as she reached the top story. Justin never minded the heat. He had himself wound around the mike stand, and she rushed across the wide room to burrow into his arms.

What was wrong. What.

She lifted her head and looked around at who else was there. Kris their bass player and Chris the drummer. But not their normal lead guitar Terry. Instead it was Henry. Or at least Henry's tousled head, his thin arms in Henry's shirt, long sleeves rolled, his thin legs in Henry's Levi's and trainers and wrinkled socks.

Feeling sick, Allie sagged against Justin's side. But she and the wizard had made their peace in Hampshire, after her fall. He hadn't meant it, killing Nick and Ginnie. Besides, he looked terrible: eyes hollow, skin pasty; bad enough she couldn't help pitying him as he reached with a trembling hand to pass a half-finished fag to Justin.

That Justin was taking from him—"Ta, mate"—but Justin was trying to quit—

She looked up at her love. From his face the wizard smiled down into her eyes.

She tore free of his embrace, scrambling backwards. No. Help, she thought. Help me. Screaming in her heart. This can't happen. Help.

You only had to ask, answered the lady.

Humming light filled Allie's head. It cleared slightly, diluting itself a bit so she could see again, and went fizzing like lemonade or ginger beer along her arms and trunk and legs and hands and feet. She found herself moving toward the other mike, a little slow and clumsy. Plenty of flex to trip over on the way, but she got there and flipped it on.

"Drone on the bass," she said. She gave the note. Kris got it, set up a sort of oscillating wave that staggered between octaves. She began without the others, her voice balanced and sure as a knife:

> The lady stands in her tower high
> As fair as any blooming rose
> The sailor stands before her door
> With his black and tarry clothes . . .

Minor chords filled the air, matching her sinuous melody. What am I *doing*, Allie wondered. Fighting, said the lady, and they were on the next verse:

> Well may you dress, you lady fair
> Into your robes as red as wine
> For I will have your maidenhead
> Before the morn at this same time.

> Away, away, bold Jackie Tar
> I'll keep me safe and sound,
> For never a man in all England
> Will bring my castle down.

Henry joined in now, and it was only him. His shaking fingers picked a skillful descant to the tune she'd chosen, but Allie watched the wizard. As the lady had expected he wanted the next verse. She let him take it:

> The sailor swore a solemn oath
> To win the lady fair
> And he became a turtledove
> To fly up in the air.

Where had that breeze come from with the windows shut tight to keep in the noise? No time to find out; her verse:

> Then she became a bright, gay hawk
> To hunt the turtle down—

Dizzy with height, she gripped the stand—

> And she has harried the sailor bold
> And driven him to the ground.

A drum fill from Chris as they wrestled in the grass, then Justin's voice sang:

> But he's turned to a cunning wolf
> A wolf both fierce and wild
> To take her in his red, red mouth
> And make her meek and mild.

Oh he would, would he? She twisted to glare at him over one feathered shoulder and shot back with:

> So then the lady's turned again
> Into a serpent vile

      Her fangs filled with a venom foul
      To poison him with her guile.

At that, of course, he dropped her. Not soon enough. She sunk her jaws into his neck, injecting him with her orders: Go. Leave. Go back home again. Bypassing all defense, direct into his soul. A dreadful weapon, dreadful beyond words; but she, she was the mightier poet.

Though of course she would have to obey her own command.

He tried to escape her and his changes came faster, two per stanza. She wrapped her tail firmly round him and clung on: wolf to running horse to lion, tiger, dragon, kraken, each metamorphosis more extravagant than the last. But hold me tight and fear not: I am your baby's father.

Finally their enemy fled. The song ended. The lady said goodbye, following him. Untangling herself from the magic she stood on two feet again, Allie at the mike. And it was Justin, only Justin looking at her now.

The rest of the band had segued to a jam. They barely noticed when she drew him off alone, walking down the stairs with him to the cooling pavement to tell him the glad news of her pregnancy. Offering joy as an excuse to weep, trumping his puzzlement and relief.

Hold me tight and fear not. And you will love your child.

#

They did, of course. They both loved their darling Mary, born in March, a Pisces. Red curls, fat cheeks, dazzling blue eyes. The band broke up and they bought a house and Allie stayed home. She recorded solo in the carriage house. Justin was there lots too.

That wasn't the problem.

He tried to blame it on drink. Only she'd given that up as soon as she knew and never started again in the year since Mary came.

Were the hallucinations worse? Hard to tell. There seemed to be a glamour over everything. All her days were filled with meaning, though she had yet to fathom the code. The lady never came back, but in her wake she left a golden hum like transparent bees flowing always now in Allie's veins. Bright sun, brisk clouds, bare branches, flooded roads, everything fascinated her. Almost she rivaled Mary in her delight at ordinary beauty. Yet there were days she must have sat blind for hours, when the shadows on the wall made huge leaps that betrayed the passage of great blocks of time.

When Justin told her, gently, that this was no way to raise a kid she had to agree. Out loud she argued as well as she could with a man who came and went sometimes in a wink. He was right, though.

So she let him take Mary to Canada. For a stay with his relatives. Though they both knew he had no intention of bringing her back.

Justin flew off with Mary, and the very next day Allie went to Wimbledon to see Mike. And to talk with Mum about what she took to stop her seizures.

Two weeks before Mary's first birthday. The snow had held off till March this year. Allie followed a plow along the motorway. White flakes continued to fall, bouncing up as the car pushed cold air over its bonnet and roof. Maybe she shouldn't have tried to drive, but Mum was so excited and she'd made so many plans. Mike's first visit home since he moved to Australia. You weren't supposed to have favorites among your kids, everyone knew that, but Mike was Mum's.

Allie had idolized Mike too when they were little. They'd been close in their way: her sneaking out behind him, following him when he went to play; Mike never letting on he knew till his pals were too deep in their game to object.

There, she'd nearly passed her turn-off. Still, she hadn't done too badly; no stuttering-film effect to speak of. A good day. Drawing in already, though. She'd left so late.

The house was dark, only an upstairs bedroom window lit. Not Mum's. And the Vauxhall absent from in front, where she always parked.

Had Allie missed them? Were they at the restaurant by now—or was it even open in this weather? She found the key beneath the planting pot and let herself in.

"Hullo?" She switched on the entry light. A pair of men's boots leaned against one another on a page from the paper. Mike at least might be there, then. Confirmation came—an indistinct question from a man further inside, it sounded like. She called Hullo again, walking towards the stairs. The light at the top wouldn't turn on.

"Allie, that you then?" Mike waited up in the shadows for her as she climbed.

"Where's Mum?" She paused on the landing, out of breath.

"She'll be along. I brought something to show you—" He left her line of sight. "—in my old room."

Allie hesitated. Why? It was here she'd seen the lady, way back before Justin, before the band, the wizard, Mary . . . before everything.

"Coming?" Mike asked. Allie went the rest of the way up. She had just registered that he'd headed in the wrong direction for his room when the carpet slipped.

Back down bumping horribly fast. No control—she hurt her hands grabbing for something to hold but her head—

She lay on her side. She could see out of one eye. The light upstairs was on now. Red slime puddled around her. "Yes, you'd better come quickly," Mike said to someone else. "She's had a terrible fall."

Allie wanted to move. Bad idea, she told herself. She smelled piss and blood, Brompton smells. "Yes," said Mike again. He gave the address. An ambulance, then. She would be all right. She heard her brother drop the phone's receiver into its cradle and then his feet came down the steps. He leaned over her. It wasn't him.

Wasn't Mike. What went away could come back. It was him, the wizard. Escaped again. Truce long since ended. "Won't be able to use you anymore after this, will she?" he asked. Leering, smug, wearing her brother's body to taunt her. No—to kill her. She wouldn't let him succeed.

With a tremendous wrench she forced herself to sit up. Then got to her feet and saw herself lying still on the floor. Not the lady. Allie herself, in her pink jumper. She'd come in two—an out-of-body experience they called this. Caused by shock.

She saw out of both eyes now. Maybe a little further behind than normal.

The wizard knew something had happened. He stood too, swiveling Mike's head, looking Allie's way again and again but apparently not seeing her.

Well. Hadn't the lady once said Allie couldn't hide from him? Wrong.

The wizard stooped beside her body once more, stuck a tentative finger in the pooled blood, licked its tip, made a face like a schoolboy given a supposed treat that turns out nasty.

The ambulance arrived. On the ride to hospital she decided she'd have to remain comatose or fake it till he left for home. Oz or the future or both or either one.

But it was hard. Mum cried, her face as empty of expression as ever but endless tears rolling down and falling disregarded off her chin.

Mike's visit went on and on and on. No one thought it odd that he put off leaving to be with his sick sister.

Allie began getting used to the way things were. Not much different. The stuttering seemed a bit worse. Time crept or sped by depending on whether anything happened. And there were other angles, new corners to the world, ways she could go somewhere else. Like a fox finding holes in a wire fence.

That was how she was able to track Justin down. In Mexico, she thought, not Alberta, judging by the scenery. Adobe walls and sunshine. So he had lied. Mary trying to gnaw the tail off a carved wooden donkey. Otherwise he was alone.

He'd lied, but soon someone would figure out where he was. They hadn't told him Allie was hurt, yet, or he would already be back home.

She wanted to touch him, but her hands streamed away as she reached for his long hair. It was no better with Mary; she might as well have been a sunbeam.

Well, then, she would just have to get back in her body. Fend off the wizard somehow. It was obvious he wasn't going anywhere on his own.

But she couldn't. She couldn't get back inside herself. Nothing worked: hovering, stretching out thin, concentrating.

All she managed to do was attract the wizard's attention.

Probably this was at night. No one else in the room. He stared right at her. "Won't be stopping me now. You and your model." He laughed under Mike's breath.

"He can hurt you through me." So the lady'd said. They were related in some way. Then would that mean Mary was too?

That could be what the wizard was waiting for. Who he was waiting for.

She called for help. Loud as she could with her heart. It had worked once before, when the lady had been inside her. Surely she would hear Allie now. Up ahead in the future, she would hear and answer her. She must know. The lady was the mightier poet. Had once defeated him. Would know how. Would tell her.

Or maybe Allie already understood what she had to do.

Then it was afternoon. They were going to pull the plug. Mum and a few others, old friends, formed a circle around her bed. She heard them talking about it.

But Allie wanted to live. To have sex with Justin in the morning on wrinkled sheets and play the perfect chord change on the piano and wipe the spit-up milk from Mary's lips. She had a child. Songs.

She had her love. She hurled herself at her body one last time, a bird flying into glass bricks.

No go.

She would have to do something. Something else besides living. Something more. Get the lady to take her in. Find the wizard up ahead in his own time, and fight him, and win.

If the lady had ridden her, Allie ought to be able to ride the lady.

Afterwards, maybe she could come back. Aim for right ahead of the funeral and make sure Mary was safe. Ride as a passenger with someone willing.

Allie let herself float up toward the ceiling. She could rise higher. In fact, it was an effort not to. An effort no longer worth making.

Below, her mother's mouth moved silently, hands folded neatly in her lap. On the ocean's other side, in an anonymous office, Justin heaved up his shoulders to disguise a sob. One hand held a piece of paper, a letter or telegram. So now he knew. His other hand held tight to Mary's arm, but he had turned his face away from her carry basket, glaring at a blank wall.

Allie could stay and haunt them.

But how would that stop the wizard?

She searched for and found the narrow road to the future: white temples, Black poets, strange beasts. And set out across the wide sky.

An Awfully Big Adventure

I'M GOING FIRST. I'm the last girl to be born, and what's left to pick by then? My oldest sister already gets to be the smart one, and the middle girl everybody decides must be the most imaginative. So I'm the brave one. Usually—except for being born—that means that I go first.

And this is why, if there has to be a reason. I go first. I don't have to know what I'm doing. Don't have to know how, why, where. I'm the first. I'm the brave one. This is an adventure. Like life. I'm going.

It all begins with a short stay in the hospital, barely overnight. Stress test in the morning, but all I can think about during that is where's my gold tennis charm necklace. My mom and my sister look everywhere, but it probably got stolen.

My tests don't prove nothin. The health care providers decide I've been experiencing anxiety attacks. Counseling is prescribed.

Couple years pass by. Turns out there's a growth on my left adrenal gland. The doctors plan on taking it out. My oldest sister talks about the friends she'll stay with in the town where they say they'll do the operation. Then something more urgent comes up: breast cancer.

It's early. Stage 0. Still, the providers decide they have to deal with that before anything else. They schedule my mastectomy.

Anesthesia. I tip into the dark. Like falling out of a canoe. The me I'm used to has been dry, always, crackers or toast; now everything I am is soaking wet. To the core. Melting apart.

I bob to the surface of the darkness. There's my sister. Nearby a woman sobs and cries about how she can't breathe. For an hour.

Finally I'm wheeled back to my room. There's dirt in the corners.

Blood keeps draining from my incision, fast and steady. We have to empty the plastic bag where it gathers every twenty minutes. The nurse lies to me and says my surgeon's not around. I get up to pee and drop through the surface again. Down under the light and air and feeling. Down. Then back up again to my mother, and back down, put there on purpose this time, to sew up the uncauterized capillary that has been pouring out blood to soak me and sink me.

Up. Light. Food. I'm home in time for Thanksgiving. I will even eat lima beans. Even beets. Coconut. Anything. Never going to turn away any blessings I'm given ever, ever again.

But I no longer trust the light the air the feeling. They went away before; I got no reason now to believe they're here to stay.

Another year passes. Time's trying to lull me. It does. I wear halter tops, tell lopsided jokes. But one day playing on the courts with my son I pull a muscle, I think. I lie down on the living room couch. Low to the water. Ripples of pain spread out from my back, lapping up against me. One hand hangs over the boat's side, trailing through the darkness, dipping in. I could sleep so long. I could sleep for always and still feel this tired.

I fight my way back to dry land. I go to the store. I talk on the phone with my oldest sister far away, ask her what remedy to take. Confess I'm out of strength. For the first time in my life. For the last.

Tell her I love her.

Don't wanna be in the hospital again, but my mother takes me anyways. The dirt in the corners is piling higher, thicker, crowding out the light. They send me home from the emergency room; they say there's nothing wrong. But there is.

A few hours later I return and the new shift realizes I have several different kinds of cancer now. One extremely rare. No good chance of a cure. They explain that, and then they carefully lay me out on the operating table, gently lowering me down.

Down. My heart has hardly been beating for weeks, they say. They want to make it beat even slower so they can work their way inside to fix things.

They can only fix them for a while. They're honest about that.

They put the sensing ends of machines on me to watch while I think. They put in drugs.

The water surges up to carry me away. To hold me under. Hold me tight. Hold me.

I'm usually the first among us three girls. Us sisters. I understand I'm the one going on ahead this time too. Into what? Into what we don't know.

Slowly I sink down. Like before, it's way too cold. Numbing me. I don't feel. No longer. No light. Don't see. No direction. No up no down no in out forward back nothing but nothing but nothing. But.

But I remember being small and closing shut my eyes and shutting them so tight, squeezing them so hard, to make the colors come and here they are and are they real and is this real is anything and am I real and am I real—

And yes.

And yes. I am. And I am going.

Under. Down. Deep.

Going.

Gone.

Ifa: Reverence, Science, and Social Technology

I WRITE SCIENCE FICTION. I practice a West African religion known as Ifa. I see no conflict between these two activities.

Many highly intelligent people have tried to define science fiction. Me too. I'm not immune to the lure of understanding what I do. The definition I came up with, the aphorism I wrote down and taped to the wall near my desk reads: "Science fiction is fiction that believes in science." That definition satisfied me at one level. Of course, it did raise the question of what it means to say that an abstraction "believes" in something. And then to say that one abstraction believes in another . . . well, that's an obscurity dangling from an additional obscurity.

Science is easier to define than science fiction. It's a system of knowing things, and it relies on forming and testing hypotheses, clearly stated suppositions about the universe. The results of these tests are supposed to be quantifiable, and the tests are supposed to be repeatable.

Is it possible to believe in science? To have faith that this one system of knowing things is correct? I think so. I'm pretty sure so. When I talk about SF believing in science, though, my meaning runs more along these lines: stories belonging to this subgenre espouse, validate, support, and extrapolate from science as a belief.

In the hit movie *Avatar*, botanist Grace Augustine defends her findings on the electrochemical network between Pandora's trees by distancing those findings from a religious belief system very much akin to my own. "This is not just pagan voodoo," she tells her corporate sponsor, reinforcing what I regard as a false dichotomy.

There are solid connections between Ifa and the realm of science: Ifa divinities sacred to certain scientific methods, technologies, and areas of study; and parallels between divination and the scientific method. The flexibility of Ifa teachings and practice makes this tradition highly adaptable and able to encompass a scientific viewpoint when called on to do so. Also, the tools of divination (both the objects used and the texts referred to), the dances, songs, prayers, and offerings with which Ifa is celebrated, can all be seen as a technological repertoire for social cultivation. After exploring these points with me, you may wish to read my science fiction story "Good Boy," available in my collection *Filter House* and on my website at www.nisishawl.com. In "Good Boy" a psychologist living on an extrasolar planet conducts experiments using an isolation tank, à la John Lilly. These experiments bring her and her detractors into contact with entities recognizable as members of the Ifa pantheon.

I'm not going to try to thoroughly define Ifa, but I'll tell you some things about it. It's animistic—that is, the Ifa universe lives and grows and changes, and it is full of subjects rather than objects. It's old. But also, it's new, because it's syncretistic—that is, it adapts itself to cultures it comes into contact with, adopting elements of them for its own purposes, thus co-opting Christianity, European paganism, and other philosophies.

As a practice, Ifa focuses on the concepts of balance and alignment. The Ifa ideal is to live a life of good character in accordance with the guidance of one's best self and the precepts of heaven. There are sacred texts, there are priests, there are offerings and ceremonies, all of which help in achieving this. There are ancestors. We all have ancestors. There are deities, and in the Ifa worldview we all enjoy interactions with these deities, whether we're aware of this or not.

So what do these ancestors and deities have to do with science and thus with science fiction? Everything.

Some ancestors, or *egun*, *were* scientists. (By the way, Ifa recognizes that not all descent is a biological matter. You can feel a strong affinity for someone—say Madame Curie—and so regard them as your ancestor.) Revering scientist ancestors affords us one way to perceive science and religion as in harmony with rather than in opposition to one another. Ifa practitioners' attitude towards egun is one of reverence, not worship: we praise the ancestors for their lives, their accomplishments, their gifts to us. We remember them, honor and respect them. But we understand their roots in humanity. We reserve worship for the superhuman.

There are said to be thousands of divinities in the Ifa pantheon. Most practitioners concentrate on a dozen or so, though, and because of space constraints I'm only going to cover three in depth in this essay.

Ogun is the *orisha*—or deity—most easily understood as relating to science, since Ogun is celebrated throughout the African diaspora as the patron of blacksmiths, of metal and metallurgy. In other words, he is a god of technology. His association with knives and other literal cutting edges leads to his association with their figurative equivalents; to invoke Ogun is to invoke frontiers, including the frontier of human knowledge.

When I first discussed the link between the orisha and science and technology with one of my elders, she spoke of computers as belonging to Ogun's realm. I noticed possible relationships between computers and other orisha, though, and as my reflections on the subject continued, between various orisha and other technologies, and between various orisha and science itself.

Exu, for instance. Exu oversees the activities of communication and translation. Ifa practitioners customarily invoke him before ceremonies because we want to be translated from the sphere of mundane concerns to the sphere of spiritual concerns, which is where most ceremonies take place. As the power of paradox, Exu makes the impossible not just possible, not just probable, but true. He's a tricky trickster, and to me the clear owner of concepts such as quantum entanglement ("spooky action at a distance") and "wavicles," concepts that defy common sense. He also rules words, one way of conveying these concepts. I pray to Exu frequently for help with communicating what I want and need to say via various programs on my computer. I pray to him every time I write a story.

Exu may have more to do with the internet than with computers per se, more to do with connection than with work in isolation. But certainly *Oya's* attributes map onto those of computers with even greater accuracy. Among the qualities these realms share: electricity; contrast; and sudden, unforeseen change.

Oya is not lightning itself—that's the purview of another orisha—but she is that which calls lightning into being: the potential for power. A goddess of boundaries, of binaries, of splitting (her name can be translated as "she tore"), she creates difference. Computers currently run on electricity, and computing operations are constructed from millions of ones and zeroes, compilations of differences. Computing and computers have reconfigured the world in which we live—and by "we" I mean *all* of us. Their advent has brought about a sudden change. It was not predicted. It occurred in a matter of years. Again, this can be seen as Oya's work. In fact, I consider all revolutions in science and technology as hers.

I could write at length of additional relationships: *Olokun*, owner of the bottom of the oceans, has ties to the study of benthic vent communities and marine biology; *Oshun*, goddess of culture, love, beauty, and luxury, to fertility science. My point is that science, the scientific method, and technological applications of scientific knowledge, are not at odds with the philosophy and worldview of Ifa. Nor are they automatically excluded from the lives of Ifa's practitioners.

Two of my coreligionists are nurses, three are writers—science fiction writers, actually—and we all use computers, we all use the internet, we all drive cars, take planes, make phone calls, and we're quite aware of the contributions of science and the scientific outlook to our well-being.

"Ah," you may say, "but the god science is a jealous god." Well, perhaps you wouldn't put it quite like that. Yet the scientific outlook *is* often supposed to be the ultimate philosophical stance, the one that uncovers what is really real. A character in my colleague Kim Stanley Robinson's novel *Galileo's Dream* tells the man now called the "Father of Modern Science" that he created "an abstraction with a concrete referent, which means that no one [can] logically deny it." But rather than denying the validity of the scientific system, logically or in some other mode, Ifa recognizes it. It doesn't do so unquestioningly. In speech and essay Ifa elders and practitioners interrogate science's basic assumptions, while emergentism, reductionism, and other scientific movements get examined and weighed for consistency and relevance to practitioners' experience.

The idea that science may reject spirituality in general, and African religious traditions in particular, as the filmic Grace Augustine does, has very little impact on its complementary acceptance by Ifa practitioners. We're used to belittlement of that sort. Christianity rejects and has always rejected African-born philosophies such as Vodun, Lucumi, and Santeria, yet these and related religions equate Christian saints with members of our pantheons. Some rituals require the use of holy water or the recitation of Bible verses. The Afrodiasporic religious outlook is deeply pragmatic; it makes use of what is useful. A scientific approach to the world is useful. Scientific knowledge is useful—also, at times, awe-inspiring and breathtakingly beautiful. What's not to like? We ain't mad at you, pretty science; don't be mad at we.

Egun and orisha are abstractions with concrete referents as well— in fact, Ifa is rich in examples of this kind of intersection. Egun once were living humans; they are abstractions evoked—and invoked—by concrete referents such as photos and personal mementos of those revered: jewelry, letters, and books, for instance. Orisha can be seen as abstractions of natural features: rivers, seas, mountains. They are invoked by shells, stones, containers of water, and images, for instance.

Early on in this essay, and in its title, I mentioned the term "social technology." I used it in a talk I gave at Stanford in 2004, "Ancestors, Ghosts, and Social Technology." If science is a system of knowledge, technology is the systematic use of that knowledge. I came to the term by the process of extrapolation. The existence of social sciences, I thought, meant that there must be social technologies. More recently, Robinson, in his Guest of Honor speech at WisCon 39 in May 2015, spoke of applying the social technology of justice to fix human-generated ecological problems. He also concludes that the tools we rely on are forms of software as well as hardware.

Viewing Ifa more as a spiritual *practice*, a cultural and social milieu, than as a theoretical construct of the cosmos, it's possible to see certain of its elements as social tools, as parts of a social technology. I want to briefly consider four of those elements now: altars, music, offerings, and divination.

Altars may be built communally or individually. They serve as portals between the visible and invisible worlds, the abstract and the concrete. In Ifa, most altars are by preference low to the ground, displaying connectedness with the earth, though altars dedicated to the orisha *Osun* are typically located on the highest flat surface available. Altars may be small and extremely simple, occupying less than a square foot of space and comprising no more than a piece of cloth, a candle, a cup of water, and an incense stick. Both water and fire model communication with the egun and the orisha: water because it is liminal, its surface a boundary between realms; and fire because it is transformational. An individual's altar facilitates personal access to the divine, much as a telescope facilitates personal access to the astronomical. Communal altars are much larger and often more complex. In addition to cloth, candle or candles, and water, they may include flowers and greenery, images of some sort (photos, paintings, drawings, statues), and representative physical loci of particular orisha, usually (but not always) ceramic pots filled with stones.

In the winter of 2010 I attended a celebration in honor of Exu. Red cloth-covered mats were laid out over an area roughly forty feet square. Green, dagger-shaped palm leaves radiated out from the altar's center. Red and white flowers—roses, lilies, gladioli—stood in vases toward the altar's back. Those attending brought their Exus from their homes to place on the cloth. These Exus are almost always a head sculpted out of laterite or clay, displayed with that Exu's accoutrements: cigars, rattles, popcorn, coins, hats, balloons, and other emblems of this orisha's powers and affinities. Three candles lit the darkened room, and a single goblet of water signified our desire to communicate with realms beyond those we customarily live in.

The process of creating an altar is a process of alignment. Building an individual altar gives physical presence to an individual's commitment to the practice of Ifa and involvement in a community of coreligionists. Building a community altar gives physical presence to the community's shared acceptance of Ifa's symbolism, values, and practices, and to its individual members' commitment to working together.

Music played an enormous part in the Exu celebration whose altar I just described. We sang, we clapped hands, we snapped fingers, we played the drums, we played the shekere. The songs were call-and-response in format. The lyrics were in Yoruba, a West African language spoken in the nation in which Ifa originates. Plenty has been written about the effectiveness of rhythm and repetition in producing trance states. That technology is well documented. I'll only add that call-and-response lends itself to simultaneously reinforcing strong feelings of community and highlighting individual experience of the community in a way that mirrors divine possession.

Offerings are another of Ifa's social technologies. Most nonpractitioners automatically associate this idea with animal sacrifice. Sometimes divination makes it clear that taking a life is required, but I can tell you that this is never done lightly. Whenever possible, the community will consume the flesh left after an animal sacrifice is made But frequently, in my experience, offerings are cowrie shells or herbal mixtures. Or they are craft objects or art projects. Recently, the practitioners I celebrate with were directed to make an offering which included a particular kind of cloth. One member had previously researched how to weave that cloth, so she created it for the community. She was given the cash portion of the offering for her personal use. When the cloth was placed before the physical locus of the orisha to whom it was dedicated, all members of the community were present to touch the cloth, appreciate its beauty, and hear how it was made. The cloth's ultimate disposition is yet to be determined, but the community as a whole, and the weaver especially, have reaped the rewards of patient diligence and the elevation of artistry. All offerings can bring practitioners together, and those that involve the sharing of creativity and knowledge are most effective in this work.

Divination is how Ifa's practitioners determine which offerings, ceremonies, and altars to perform and make. In divination, both querent and diviner try to cast aside preconceived notions of the truth of a particular assertion, just as scientists do when conducting research. Much thought is given to which questions to ask and how to frame them to reduce ambiguity.

Diviners consult egun and orisha—especially the patron of divination, *Orunmila*. Anyone can be a diviner using the appropriate method for their role as a practitioner. These methods include using four cowries to generate five answers along a yes/no axis, culminating in the use of a round tray and sixteen *ikin* (palm nuts) to consult a sacred text comprising 256 chapters, with the four cowries reserved in this mode for questions arising from the original results. Interpretation of the sacred text is constantly being refined through notes diviners make on its application and the subsequent experiences of querents. So actual events contribute to how these chapters are understood, which seems to me akin to the way in which actual data elicited by scientific experiments influence future repetitions and redesign of those experiments. As Robinson said during his remarks at the symposium where I gave the speech this essay is based on, science "pings" its environment, re-forming its model of the world based on what it finds. And this is what Ifa divination does as well.

I also see a resemblance between the scientific method and the four-cowries and ikin methods of divination in that both modes of investigation require forming a hypothesis and testing it against empirical evidence—the results of an experiment or the results of randomly casting the cowrie shells or ikin. In the case of the four-cowries method, I may ask if it would be to my benefit to move into a shared housing situation with a woman I've known for twenty-five years. The possible responses can be translated roughly as: "Oh, yeah!" "Yes," "Maybe—with certain conditions," "Probably not," and "No way!" When receiving a maybe answer, further divination is required, necessitating further hypotheses and testing.

Though the title of the symposium where I originally spoke on this topic was "Competing Cosmologies," I refrained in that speech and refrain here again from outlining an overall Ifa cosmology. Such things exist and are important and possible to teach and learn. Yet my attitude toward Ifa cosmologies, and the attitudes of others as I've encountered them, mirrors the attitude of professional scientists toward science as described by Robinson in his many essays and interviews on the basic character of science: less a case of practitioners discovering natural laws and offering them as explication for the world than one of recognizing a "startling adherence" to certain patterns. This is yet another similarity between these systems, in my mind: their lack of arrogant assumptions in relation to what is observed.

These are some of the ways I see science and religion—or at any rate, *my* religion—in harmony with each other. Which should begin to explain to you how I can write in a genre I conceive of as "believing" in an approach to the world many would say is at odds with *all* religious philosophies. I understand the stances of science and Ifa as mutually supportive in the case of reverence for historical scientific figures, as mutually validating in the case of respect for objective observation and verifiable models of practical reality, and as mutually expansive in the case of concern for the extent of human knowledge.

What if my understanding of the mutuality of these systems could be more widely adopted? What would be the implications for science fiction and its criticism? For establishing the genre's parameters?

Perhaps in addition to the categories of "hard" and "soft" science fiction a new one labeled "ethereal SF" would be born, focusing on science derived from spiritually mandated investigations rather than discoveries in conventional physics or biology. Or perhaps we'd witness the fading of literature's taxonomical division between science fiction and its more widely accepted and well-to-do sister genres, fantasy and magical realism. Already this division is problematic, questioned by many authors and thoughtful readers—particularly those familiar with Ifa and other religions rooted in indigenous worldviews.

For a critic, this fading of divisions could mean expecting equivalent levels of rigor and consistency from all imaginative fiction and according all examples of it equivalent intellectual respect. For the genre's audience, it could lead to a higher regard for an author's demonstrated ability to please them than for the marketing label attached to that author's newest work. For brick-and-mortar booksellers, it could involve the formalization of broader categories within the genre—or of none at all. Conversely for publishers and online booksellers, it could lead to narrower ones: the in-the-tradition-of-Ray-Bradbury category versus the category of new-authors-like-Shirley-Jackson, for instance.

For an editor such as myself, the dissolution of imagined incompatibilities between science/science fiction and spirituality/fantasy could remove the distraction of considering which genre subheading I'm drawing on to populate the anthology or magazine I'm curating. We editors could focus instead on other criteria (verisimilitude, audacity, originality, wit, etc.), making our selections along axes having nothing to do with a contrived dichotomy between a given work's reliance on either scientific or religious paradigms.

For an author—again, such as myself—the initial consequences of adopting this mind-set are also subtractive, getting rid of hampering definitions. But losing the restrictive notion that science and religion are antagonists can easily increase writers' options and thus our creative output. Accommodating these supposedly mutually exclusive viewpoints allows us to speak with the voices of those who accept both as valid. It allows us to explore their interrelationship and to reflect on what it is our characters seek from each, and how, and why. It helps us address the universe as the whole that it is.

If you'd like a concrete example of the way this works for me, I refer you to my stories—in particular to the aforementioned "Good Boy," as it deals specifically with how an individual and a community resolve their conflict over this very matter.

"The Fly in the Sugar Bowl"

Nisi Shawl interviewed by Terry Bisson

What's the deal with you and dolls?
Dolls are how we learn to be people. We pretend we're human with dolls so as to get the hang of it. I'm still paying attention, still being educated.

What (or who) drew (or pushed) you into science fiction?
I can't remember a time when I *wasn't* into science fiction or some form of fiction operating outside consensus reality. Early influences include Rod Serling's *Twilight Zone* series, Ruthven Todd's Space Cat books, *The Wonderful Flight to the Mushroom Planet* by Eleanor Cameron, *Mary Poppins* (and all the sequels), *Tatsinda* by Elizabeth Enright, *A Wrinkle in Time* by Madeleine L'Engle, and everything Edward Eager ever wrote. When I was in sixth grade, I persuaded the librarians at the downtown Kalamazoo branch to let me read books shelved in the adult SF section and discovered Ray Bradbury, Theodore Sturgeon, et al., and it was all over.

What period in history interests you most?
Currently I'm most interested in two periods: the late Victorian/ Edwardian era and the late 1950s/early 1960s. *Everfair* was set in the first period, but even before I began work on it, I was drawn to that time as one of enormous change and consequential choices. Regarding the second period, I've written two-thirds of a novella, "The Day and Night Books of Mardou Fox," set in the 1960s, which

is also the background for my forthcoming middle-grade fantasy, *Speculation*. And I set a flash story there too. It's called "More than Nothing," and it's part of Tor.com's *Nevertheless, She Persisted* anthology.

I suppose part of my fascination with that time stems from my personal connection—I was born in 1955 and have memories of my life from nursery school onward. Also, though, it was an amazingly optimistic time for black people. We were making progress in terms of our civil rights, our culture was strong and beautiful, particularly our music—the Blue Note jazz scene, Motown—just a magical historical moment.

What tech device do you find most helpful? Least?
Most useful has got to be my smart phone. I don't have to cart around a laptop to read my email, access documents, watch movies, accomplish lots of laptop-centric tasks. Least useful tech device? That's a harder pick. If it's not useful, I'm not using it, and I tend not to think about things I don't use. I suppose dishwashers qualify. I eschew online calendars also. Which is most unuseful? Hard to judge.

What poets do you read for fun or pleasure?
Umm, none? If poetry is thrust upon me—if I come across it in a mixed-format book or someone dedicates a piece to me—I may read and enjoy it. Generally, though, I find it too intense, even though I've been known to write it. Reading a poem is like drinking a tumblerful of lemon juice.

The exception is song lyrics. Those I can handle.

Does science model the universe or the human mind?
Oh, science can't help but model the human mind, because it's born of the human mind. It's probably the closest we'll get to modeling the universe as well, though.

My Jeopardy *item (I provide the answer, you provide the question): Writing while white.*
What's the default setting for authors in this place and time?

One sentence on each, please: Jordan Peele, Paul Robeson, Alison Bechdel.
Sure would like to meet Jordan Peele and hang with him for a day. Paul Robeson has all my love and respect. (Did you know I named a character in my cyberpunk story "Deep End" after him?) Does Alison Bechdel know Samuel R. Delany—and if not, does she want to?

What car do you drive? I ask this of everyone.
I drive a 2018 Honda Fit. I bought it when my mom was still alive because at the time I drove a standard (stick shift) 1996 Honda Accord, and she couldn't operate the clutch. She had a partially paralyzed left leg, so I bought my first automatic with her physical abilities in mind. I had once borrowed a friend's Fit—an earlier model—and I was impressed with its carrying capacity and ease of parking. The friend reported it as being nicely reliable too. My Fit's not a real smooth ride, and there's a wide window stanchion that impinges on my view when I look out the left side, but otherwise I like it. It's painted a shiny, metallic blue and bombed with crow shit. I named it Melina, after the Greek singer/actress/activist Melina Mercouri.

How did you research Everfair*? Was it hard to do or hard to quit?*
Researching *Everfair* was hard in that there wasn't much to go on when it came to certain areas of knowledge. Particularly scarce was information on the indigenous people of the Upper Congo in the 1890s—people who were decimated and, in some cases, completely wiped out. But the research was fun and also deeply rewarding. I created several characters I wouldn't have thought of, basing them on surprise facts.

And some of my research was deeply physical too. In addition to reading books and articles, I ate relevant foods, listened to relevant music, and collected and pored over photos, maps, and floor plans.

My method is research-as-you-go, which is why I can't use the sorts of retreats that cut you off from the internet, the starting point of many of my inquiries. Questions come up as I write, and the answers I find shape the story's subsequent lines, paragraphs, pages . . . That thing where you put in a note telling yourself to add a description later? I don't do that. For me, that doesn't work. I need it all to be there. One detail leads to another.

What's with the sequel?
I'm not sure what you're asking. It exists. Or rather, it will; there will be a sequel. My working title is *Kinning*. I gave an outline to Tor and I signed a contract and there's a deadline. The sequel concerns infectious empathy, community, hierarchy, and a struggle for succession. I'm going to try to limit myself to only four viewpoint characters: Tink, Bee-Lung, Princess Mwadi, and Prince Ilunga. But Rima, Rosemary, and Laurie will be prominently featured too.

What's the origin of Writing the Other? *Is it a book or a class? What if you're writing a book about someone who isn't a writer?*
Writing the Other: A Practical Approach is a book based on a class based on an essay based on something I overheard a friend say twenty-seven years ago. The book was published in 2005, and there've been many classes derived from and associated with it since then. We hope to do an update soon.

Were you ever part of fandom?
Sure. I would say I was part of fandom when I attended my very first convention. Confusion, it was called, and the guest of honor was C.J. Cherryh, whom I idolized. I dressed up as her, in fact: streaked silver

through my afro and donned a flight suit like one of her characters. I also attended a World Fantasy Convention in Chicago and got fed cookies by Gene Wolfe.

We're talking the 1980s and '90s. At that time I was an exception; hardly anyone of African descent went to cons besides me. For years and years I was what Nalo Hopkinson calls "the fly in the sugar bowl." I used to go up to every black person I saw at any given convention, introduce myself, shake their hand. Because I could. Because there would be maybe two or three of us among a thousand plus white attendees. Couple of East Asians if the scene was ultra-diverse.

Since Race Fail, which gave rise to Con or Bust, that has changed. At a recent WisCon there were over a hundred nonwhite attendees out of around eight hundred total. No way I could introduce myself to every single one.

Yet fandom still has profound issues when it comes to racial equity. I have still felt unwelcome and frozen out at conventions. The behavior I have problems with isn't necessarily explicitly racist. It doesn't have to be, though, if I've become sensitized to that sort of thing by fending off multiple microaggressions every day.

You mention "Race Fail, which gave rise to Con or Bust." Huh?
Con or Bust, a nonprofit giving travel grants to fans of color attending science fiction conventions, grew out of its founders' dissatisfaction with the resources available to POC wishing to make their participation in fandom more visible. Race Fail, remember, was about white fans doubting the existence of nonwhite fans. By helping nonwhite fans attend cons (which are crucial in the construction of SFFH's community), Con or Bust literally changed the face of that community.

What is the filter in Filter House?
It's a biological means of feeding oneself. See, there are these very small sea creatures called appendicularians, and they create "filter houses"

out of mucus to trap food particles and funnel them into their bellayz. A filter house is like a very tiny, three-dimensional, underwater spider web. As an appendicularian grows in size, it creates larger and larger filter houses for a better fit. The discards become a large part of the constant fall of organic matter sinking down through the ocean and providing sustenance to deep layers where light isn't so readily available. (This foodfall is also known as "marine snow.")

I guess I was thinking of the book as collecting stories the way a real-life filter house collects food. And then it detaches and drifts into the depths of your mind? Something like that.

Were you ever published in the Whole Earth Catalog? *I was.*
You got me there. My most outstanding hippy cred is taking a shit with Wavy Gravy.

Your move to Seattle is celebrated (on your website) as: "This mermaid has returned to the sea." Huh? Aren't you from Michigan?
I lived on the Atlantic when I spent eight months in Scotland. For me, those waters are haunted. My godmother, Luisah Teish, attributes this to ancestral memory. Thousands of African captives jumped or were thrown into the Atlantic Ocean. Tossed overboard alive when deemed unprofitable as merchandise. Escaping to their deaths from stinking hellholds. The waters of the Pacific missed out on absorbing those horrors, so it's to them I turn for my salt and tides. Which, apparently, I need.

Ecologically speaking, there are many similarities between the Seattle area and my home state of Michigan. Flora, fauna, at times even climate. And we're far north here, bordering on Canada. I like that. I'm used to it. Feels like I can leave the country by walking in the right direction.

There's more to it than that, of course. I attended two writing programs here back when I was still based in the Midwest. I did divination before deciding to move and was told in resoundingly definite terms that this was the place. But the previous two paragraphs are true enough for jazz.

Did you know Octavia Butler? What do people today get wrong about her?
I did indeed know Octavia and got to hang out with her a bunch while we both lived in Seattle. We went to restaurants, shops, and plays together, among other expeditions. We talked on the phone. I had her over for dinner, and she reciprocated.

The thing I find most annoying and ignorant these days is when lesbians claim her as one of their own. Listen, unless she was deeply, deeply closeted, Octavia was a heterosexual. I'm queer—currently preferring they/them pronouns and identifying also as bisexual. Octavia was no homophobe, but in all our many conversations she never so much as hinted to me that women attracted her. People grow, and sexuality can change and develop. At the time of her death, however, and as far as she was concerned for her entire life prior, she was not a lesbian. Period.

As you approach our present in your "Crash Course in the History of Black Science Fiction," you celebrate "the emergence of self- and small press publishing as a black SF force to be reckoned with." Really? Isn't this just making the best of a bad thing?
Ninety percent of being black is about making the best of a bad thing. Case in point: chitterlings.

Self- and small press publishing, though, are definitely on the rise. Their moment has come. They're far more nimble than traditional publishing houses and thus able to more quickly capitalize on niches and trends just rising to prominence. Case in point: PM.

Who is Carl Brandon?
Carl Brandon was a hoax. Terry Carr and Pete Graham perpetrated him on fandom in the 1940s and '50s as a means of rendering

the community less blindingly white. When we founded the Carl Brandon Society (CBS) in 1999, Ian K. Hageman suggested it as a suitable namesake. You can learn more in Carr's essay, which Jeanne Gomoll reprinted in the fundraising book titled *Carl Brandon* she put together for the CBS.

Ever go to Burning Man?
No, but I've done dogsitting for people who went. Does that count?

In the 1970s and '80s I attended the annual Rainbow Family Gatherings, which I categorize as Burning Man precursors.

You're a critic as well as a writer. What's your take on cyberpunk? High fantasy? Mundanity?
I have written cyberpunk and enjoyed reading it—though mostly what I like challenges any even temporary status quo associated with the genre. I mean, back in 1992, people were already convening a symposium about its overness, which made me rather sad, as I hadn't yet gotten a crack at smacking it down. It was dying without my hand on the murder weapon.

My cyberpunk stories are basically the six published so far in my Making Amends series: "Deep End," "In Colors Everywhere," "Like the Deadly Hands," "The Best Friend We Never Had," "Living Proof," and "The Mighty Phin." I plan two more: "Over a Long Time Ago" and another still sans title. I suppose "Walk like a Man," included in this book, qualifies as well.

I haven't answered your question, though, have I? Eileen Gunn's "Computer Friendly" is the kind of cyberpunk I admire and want more of. That help?

"High fantasy" gives me the heebie-jeebies as a term. What's it higher than? What's it high on? I do love some literature that has been classified as high fantasy—most notably Lord Dunsany's novel *The King of Elfland's Daughter*. *Lilith*, by George MacDonald, fits in there as well, right? It's a favorite of mine too. Lyrical prose is one of the things I appreciate about so-called high fantasy. Its focus on the upper classes is one of the things I do not appreciate about it.

Your third named category, Mundanity, I'm going to assume refers to the movement founded by Geoff Ryman, in which traditional SF tropes such as faster-than-light travel are bypassed in favor of futuristic elements actually extrapolated from current scientific knowledge. I think it's a noble concept, and it has produced some beautiful, laudable work, such as Ryman's *V.A.O.* Tragedy's more believable against a rigorously constructed background.

Where does Afrofuturism fit into all this? Or does it?
Afrofuturism is not a subgenre of SFFH, like the things you asked me about. It's a means of encompassing many different genres and subgenres. It's an aesthetic movement rather than a set of guidelines for ways to construct or read a story. Authors Milton Davis and Balogun Ojetade have named certain parallel subgenres in light of their contributors' Afrofuturist bent: steamfunk, sword-and-soul, etc. I call *Everfair* AfroRetroFuturist, stitching together the "retrofuturist" name steampunks give themselves with Afrofuturism. No need to choose one over the other.

Ever done a graphic novel (comic book)?
No, I haven't. I'd like to, though. My friend, artist Steve Lieber, thought I should do a script for my Louisa May Alcott send-up, "The Tawny Bitch." Comic books are such a different art form! I figured out a lot about the differences just drafting an outline to work from.

Everfair would be a cool comic, wouldn't it?

Do you follow (or attend) Superhero movies? Online games? What do you do for fun?
Answer questions like these.

What question were you hoping I would ask that I didn't?
I'm not sure how this could have been framed as a question, but I was hoping to talk a bit about how, as a teen, my friends would have deemed me rabidly apolitical. My first true love destroyed draft records with fake blood attacks and organized a months-long sit-in at the Post Office. His best buddy fought cops in the streets of Chicago at the 1968 Democratic Convention with nothing but a wet bandana between him and clouds of tear gas. By contrast, my most radical act as an adolescent was probably playing a wooden flute in a bank lobby.

Even though some of my earliest memories include walking picket lines with my parents, for a long while those sorts of actions simply were not my jam. Poetry, magic, those were my preferred modes of revolution.

Nowadays, of course, I'm up for all of them. To paraphrase Marlon Brando's character in *The Wild One*: How am I rebelling against the patriarchy? "How many ways ya got?"

Bibliography

Books

Everfair, Tor Books, New York, 2016.

Filter House, Aqueduct Press, Seattle, 2008.

Writing the Other: A Practical Guide, with Cynthia Ward, Aqueduct
    Press, Seattle, 2005.

Anthologies

New Suns: Original Speculative Fiction by People of Color, Solaris,
    Oxford, 2019.

Stories for Chip: A Tribute to Samuel R. Delany, coedited with Bill
    Campbell, Rosarium, Greenbelt, MD, 2015.

*Strange Matings: Science Fiction, Feminism, African American Voices, and
    Octavia E. Butler*, coedited with Rebecca J. Holden, Aqueduct
    Press, Seattle, 2013.

The WisCon Chronicles 5: Writing and Racial Identity, Aqueduct Press,
    Seattle, 2011.

Fiction

"Evens," in *The Obama Inheritance*, Three Rooms Press, New York,
    October 2017.

"Vulcanization," in *The Best American Science Fiction and Fantasy*,
    Mariner, Boston, October 2017 (reprint) (*Everfair* adjacent).

"Sunshine of Your Love," in *The Sum of Us*, Laksa Media, Calgary,
    Alberta, September 2017.

"The Colors of Money," in *Sunvault*, Upper Rubber Boot Books, Nashville, August 2017 (an *Everfair* sequel).

"Sun River," in *Clockwork Cairo*, Twopenny Books, UK, June 2017 (an *Everfair* sequel).

"More than Nothing," for Tor.com's *Nevertheless She Persisted* anthology, March 2017.

"Queen of Dirt," in *Apex* magazine no. 93, February 2017.

"Slippernet," for *Slate* magazine's Trump Story Project, February 2017, Slate.com.

"Lazzrus," in *Upside Down: Inverted Tropes in Storytelling*, Apex Publications, Lexington, KY, December 2016.

"Luisah's Church," in *Dark Discoveries* no. 36, Journalstone, Fall 2016.

"Just Between Us," in *Words* magazine, Hex Publishers, Erie, CO, December 2016 (reprint).

"The Pragmatical Princess," in *The Dragon Super Pack*, Wilder Press, November 2016 (reprint).

"Like the Deadly Hands," in *Analog* 136, no. 12, December 2016.

"Cruel Sistah," in the *People of Colo(u)r Destroy Horror* special issue of *Nightmare* magazine, October 2016 (reprint).

"The Mighty Phin," in *Cyber World*, Hex Publishers, Erie, CO, September 2016.

"Deep End," in *The Right Way to Be Crippled and Naked*, Cinco Puntos Press, El Paso, September 2016 (reprint).

"An Awfully Big Adventure," in *An Alphabet of Embers*, Stone Bird Press, Lawrence, KS, July 2016.

"White Dawn," in *Procyon Press Science Fiction Anthology*, Procyon Press, San Francisco, July 2016 (reprint).

"The Mighty Phin," for Tor.com's Cyberpunk Week, June 2016 (reprint).

"Jamaica Ginger" (with Nalo Hopkinson), in *The Best Science Fiction and Fantasy of the Year*, Vol. 10, Solaris, Oxford, May 2016 (reprint).

"Street Worm," in *Street Magicks*, Prime Books, Germantown, MD, April 2016 (reprint).

"Salt on the Dance Floor," in *Not Your Average Monster*, Vol. 2, Bloodshot Books, Sharon, MA, February 2016 (reprint).

"Vulcanization," in *Nightmare* magazine no. 40, January 2016.

"Jamaica Ginger," in *Stories for Chip*, Rosarium Publishing, Greenbelt, MD, August 2015.

"At the Huts of Ajala," in *See the Elephant* no. 1, Metaphysical Circus Press, July 2015 (reprint).

"Walk like a Man," in *Bahamut* no. 1, Underland Press, June 2015.

"A Beautiful Stream," in *Cranky Ladies of History*, FableCroft, Mawson, Australia, March 2015.

"The Tawny Bitch," in *The Mammoth Book of Gaslit Romance*, edited by Ekaterina Sedia, Robinson, London, November 2014 (reprint).

"Street Worm," in *Streets of Shadows*, edited by Maurice Broaddus and Jerry Gordon, Alliteration Ink, Dayton, OH, September 2014.

"The Return of Chérie," in *The Mammoth Book of Steampunk Adventures*, edited by Sean Wallace, Robinson, London, September 2014 (reprint).

"Promised," in *Steampunk World*, edited by Sarah Hans, Alliteration Ink, Dayton, OH, June 2014.

"White Dawn," in *Athena's Daughters*, edited by Jean Rabe, Silence in the Library, Washington, DC, May 2014.

"Wallamelon," in *Magic City: Recent Spells*, edited by Paula Guran, Prime Books, Germantown, MD, April 2014 (reprint).

"Lupine," in *Once Upon a Time*, edited by Paula Guran, Prime Books, Gaithersburg, MD, November 2013.

"Red Matty," in *Strange Horizons* 2013 Fund Drive Special Issue, September 2013, strangehorizons.com.

"Otherwise," in *Heiresses of Russ 2013: The Year's Best Lesbian Speculative Fiction*, Lethe Press, Maple Shade, NJ, August 2013 (reprint).

"The Five Petals of Thought," in *Missing Links and Secret Histories*, Aqueduct Press, Seattle, May 2012.

"In Colors Everywhere," in *The Other Half of the Sky*, Candlemark and Gleam, Bennington, VT, April 2012.

"Salt on the Dance Floor," in *Beast Within 3: Oceans Unleashed*, edited by
Jennifer Brozek, Graveside Tales, Lakeside, AZ, December 2012.

"Extremiades," in *Like a Coming Wave: Oceanic Erotica*, edited by
Andrea Trask, Circlet Press, Cambridge, MA, December 2012.

"In Blood and Song," in collaboration with Michael Ehart, in *Dark
Faith 2: Invocations*, edited by Maurice Broaddus and Jerry
Gordon, Apex Publications, Lexington, KY, August 2012.

"Honorary Earthling," at *Expanded Horizons*, December 2011,
expandedhorizons.net.

"Otherwise," in *Brave New Love*, Running Press, Philadelphia,
December 2011.

"Black Betty," at *Crossed Genres*, December 2011, crossedgenres.com.

"Beyond the Lighthouse," in *River*, edited by Alma Alexander, Dark
Quest Books, Howell, NJ, November 2011.

"The Last of Cherie," in *Steam Powered 2: More Lesbian Steampunk*,
Torquere Press, Round Rock, TX, November 2011.

"Just Between Us," in *Phantom Drift: A Journal of New Fabulism* no. 1,
Fall 2011.

"The Pragmatical Princess," in *Fantasy* magazine no. 53, August 9, 2011
(reprint).

"Something More," in *Something More and More*, Aqueduct Press,
Seattle, May 2011.

"Pataki," in *Something More and More*, Aqueduct Press, Seattle, May
2011 (reprint).

"Pataki," at *Strange Horizons*, Part One, April 4, 2011; Part Two, April
11, 2011, strangehorizons.com.

"To the Moment," at *Reflection's Edge*, November 2007, reflectionsedge.com.

"Little Horses," in *Detroit Noir*, Akashic Books, New York, November
2007.

"Women of the Doll," in *GUD Magazine*, Laconia, NH, Fall 2007.

"Deep End," in *2007 Think GalactiCon Discussion Primer*, Think
Galactic Literary Cooperative, Chicago, July 14, 2007.

"But She's Only a Dream," at *Trabuco Road*, March 2007, trabucoroad.com.

"The Snooted One," at *Farrago's Wainscot*, January 2007, farragoswainscot.com.

"Cruel Sistah," in *Asimov's Science Fiction* magazine 29, no. 10–11, October/November 2005; *The Year's Best Fantasy & Horror* no. 19, St. Martin's Press, New York, August 2006.

"Matched," at *The Infinite Matrix*, May 2005, infinitematrix.net (excerpt from the novel *The Blazing World*, cosponsored by the Office of Arts and Cultural Affairs).

"Wonder-Worker-of-the-World," in *Reflection's Edge*, May 2005.

"Wallamelon," in *Aeon Speculative Fiction* no. 3, March 2005.

"Deep End," in *So Long Been Dreaming: Postcolonial Science Fiction and Fantasy*, edited by Nalo Hopkinson and Uppinder Mehan, Arsenal Pulp Press, Vancouver, BC, 2004.

"Looking for Lilith," in *Lenox Avenue* magazine no. 1, July 2004

"Maggies," in *Dark Matter: Reading the Bones*, Warner Books, New York, January 2004

"Momi Watu," in *Strange Horizons*, August 18, 2003.

"The Tawny Bitch," in *Mojo: Conjure Stories*, Warner Books, New York, April 2003.

"Vapors," in *Wet: More Aqua Erotica*, Mary Anne Mohanraj (editor), Three Rivers Press, New York, 2002.

"Shiomah's Land," in *Asimov's Science Fiction* magazine 25, no. 3, March 2001.

"At the Huts of Ajala," in *Dark Matter: A Century of Speculative Fiction from the African Diaspora*, New York, July 2000, Warner Books. Also reprinted in *Filter House*.

"The Pragmatical Princess," in *Asimov's Science Fiction* magazine 23, no. 1, January 1999.

"Down in the Flood," in *PanGaia*, Summer 1998.

"Down in the Flood," in *Daughters of Nyx*, Fall 1996.

"The Rainses'," in *Isaac Asimov's Ghosts*, Ace, New York, August 1995.

"The Rainses'," in *Asimov's Science Fiction* magazine 19, no. 4–5, April 1995.

"I Was a Teenage Genetic Engineer," in *Semiotext(e) SF*, Semiotext(e), New York, April 1989.

Nonfiction

"My One-and-Only Octavia," in *Luminescent Threads: Connections to Octavia E. Butler*, Twelfth Planet Press, Yokine, WA, August 2017.

"All My Relations," in *The WisCon Chronicles 11: Trials by Whiteness*, Aqueduct Press, Seattle, May 2017.

"Golden Ages," at Fantasy Café, April 2017, fantasybookcafe.com.

"Peter Pan and *Everfair*," at *Unbound Worlds*, October 2016, unboundworlds.com.

"Representing My Equals," at the *Tor/Forge* blog, September 2016, torforgeblog.com.

"*Everfair*: The Big Idea," at *Whatever*, September 2016, whatever.scalzi. com.

"She Smells Tea Spells in the Steam Clouds," at Tor.com, September 2016.

"Five Books about Loving Everybody," at Tor.com, August 2016.

"Ones and Twos and Rarely Threes," at *Fireside Magazine* site, July 2016, firesidefiction.com.

"Our Queer Roundtable" (with A.J. Odasso, anna anthropy, Rose Fox, Vanessa Rose Phin, and Cynthia Ward), at *Strange Horizons*, July 25, 2016, strangehorizons.com.

"The Best and Worst of Writing Cyberpunk," for Tor.com's Cyberpunk Week, June 2016.

"The People Men Don't See," in the *People of Colo(u)r Destroy Science Fiction* special issue of *Lightspeed* magazine, June 2016.

"Across the Lies of Space and Time," in *The WisCon Chronicles 10*, Aqueduct Press, Seattle, May 2016.

"A Crash Course in the History of Black Science Fiction," in *Fantastic Stories of the Imagination* no. 232, January/February 2016.

"IGY," in *Shattered Prism* no. 1, Rosarium Publishing, December 2015.

Foreword to Rob Darnell, *Ruins Excavation*, Hadley Rille Books, Overland Park, KS, November 2015.

"Family Ties," in *The WisCon Chronicles 9*, Aqueduct Press, Seattle, May 2015.

"Unqualified," in *The Cascadia Subduction Zone* 5, no. 1, Aqueduct Press, Seattle, January 2015.

"Power Begets Power," in *The WisCon Chronicles 8: Re-Generating WisCon*, edited by Rebecca J. Holden, Aqueduct Press, Seattle, May 2014.

"Reviewing the Other: Like Dancing about Architecture," in *Strange Horizons*, March 24, 2014, strangehorizons.com.

"Past the World's End: *Walk to the End of the World* by Suzy McKee Charnas," in *The Cascadia Subduction Zone*, Aqueduct Press, Seattle, January 2014.

"A Brave and Contrary Thing: Review of *AfroSF: Science Fiction by African Writers*," in *Paradoxa 25: Africa SF*, Paradoxa, Vashon Island, WA, December 2013.

"Into the Canny Valley," introduction to Jane Irwin's graphic novel *The Clockwork Game*, Fiery Studios, Kalamazoo, MI, December 2013.

"Invisible Inks: On Black SF Authors and Disability," in *The WisCon Chronicles 7: Shattering Ableist Narratives*, Aqueduct Press, Seattle, May 2013.

"Unbending Gender," in *Writers Workshop of Science Fiction and Fantasy*, Seventh Star Press, Lexington, KY, April 2013.

"What I Want: WisCon 35 Guest of Honor Speech," in *The WisCon Chronicles 6: Futures of Feminism and Fandom*, Aqueduct Press, Seattle, May 2012.

"Annunciation," introduction to *Ancient, Ancient: Stories*, Aqueduct Press, Seattle, May 2012.

"Transbluency: An Antiprojection Chant," in *The Moment of Change*, May 2012, Aqueduct Press, Seattle (poem).

"Cookies and Kindness: Meeting Gene Wolfe," in the program for the
Chicago Literary Hall of Fame's Evening to Honor Gene Wolfe,
March 17, 2012.

"I Hear a Different Frontier," at the *Future Fire* blog, edited by Djibril
al-Ayad, June 11, 2012, press.futurefire.net.

The WisCon Chronicles 5: Writing and Racial Identity, Aqueduct Press,
Seattle, May 2011 (editor).

"How to Save the World, One Story at a Time," in *Something More and
More*, May 2011, Aqueduct Press, Seattle (reprint).

"Because We Are All So Royal," in *Something More and More*, May
2011, Aqueduct Press, Seattle (reprint).

"Race, Again, Still," at *Strange Horizons*, April 4, 2011, strangehorizons.
com.

"Solitude and Souls," in *80! Memories and Reflections on Ursula K. Le
Guin*, Aqueduct Press, Seattle, October 2010.

"Because We Are All So Royal," *The WisCon Chronicles 2*, Aqueduct
Press, Seattle, May 2008.

"The Third Parable," in *Potlatch 17 Program*, Seattle, February 29, 2008.

"Dry Eyes," in *The WisCon Chronicles 1*, Aqueduct Press, Seattle, May
2007.

"To Jack Kerouac, to Make Much of Space and Time," in *Talking Back:
Epistolary Fantasies*, edited by L. Timmel Duchamp, Aqueduct
Press, Seattle, March 2006.

About the Author

NISI SHAWL WROTE THE 2016 Nebula finalist and Tiptree Honor novel *Everfair*, an alternate history in which the Congo overthrows King Leopold II's genocidal regime, and the 2008 Tiptree Award–winning story collection *Filter House*. In 2005 they cowrote *Writing the Other: A Practical Approach*, now the standard text on diverse character representation in the imaginative genres, and the basis of their online and in-person classes of the same name. They are a founder of the inclusivity-focused Carl Brandon Society and served on the Clarion West Writers Workshop's board of directors for twenty years.

Shawl's dozens of acclaimed stories have appeared in *Analog* and *Asimov's* magazines, among other publications. Their "*Everfair*-adjacent" story "Vulcanization" was included in Houghton Mifflin Harcourt's *The Best American Science Fiction and Fantasy 2017* and has been translated into Polish. They edited *New Suns: Original Speculative Fiction by People of Color* and in the past has edited and coedited many more anthologies, such as *Stories for Chip: A Tribute to Samuel R. Delany* and *Strange Matings: Science Fiction, Feminism, African American Voices, and Octavia E. Butler*, both finalists for the Locus Award. Their middle-grade historical fantasy *Speculation* is coming out in 2020 from Lee & Low. Currently they are writing *Kinning*, an *Everfair* sequel.

FRIENDS OF

PM

These are indisputably momentous times—the financial system is melting down globally and the Empire is stumbling. Now more than ever there is a vital need for radical ideas.

In the years since its founding—and on a mere shoestring—PM Press has risen to the formidable challenge of publishing and distributing knowledge and entertainment for the struggles ahead. With hundreds of releases to date, we have published an impressive and stimulating array of literature, art, music, politics, and culture. Using every available medium, we've succeeded in connecting those hungry for ideas and information to those putting them into practice.

Friends of PM allows you to directly help impact, amplify, and revitalize the discourse and actions of radical writers, filmmakers, and artists. It provides us with a stable foundation from which we can build upon our early successes and provides a much-needed subsidy for the materials that can't necessarily pay their own way. You can help make that happen—and receive every new title automatically delivered to your door once a month—by joining as a Friend of PM Press. And, we'll throw in a free T-shirt when you sign up.

Here are your options:
- $30 a month: Get all books and pamphlets plus 50% discount on all webstore purchases
- $40 a month: Get all PM Press releases (including CDs and DVDs) plus 50% discount on all webstore purchases
- $100 a month: Superstar—Everything plus PM merchandise, free downloads, and 50% discount on all webstore purchases

For those who can't afford $30 or more a month, we have Sustainer Rates at $15, $10, and $5. Sustainers get a free PM Press T-shirt and a 50% discount on all purchases from our website.

Your Visa or Mastercard will be billed once a month, until you tell us to stop. Or until our efforts succeed in bringing the revolution around. Or the financial meltdown of Capital makes plastic redundant. Whichever comes first.

PM Press was founded at the end of 2007 by a small collection of folks with decades of publishing, media, and organizing experience. PM Press co-conspirators have published and distributed hundreds of books, pamphlets, CDs, and DVDs. Members of PM have founded enduring book fairs, spearheaded victorious tenant organizing campaigns, and worked closely with bookstores, academic conferences, and even rock bands to deliver political and challenging ideas to all walks of life. We're old enough to know what we're doing and young enough to know what's at stake.

We seek to create radical and stimulating fiction and nonfiction books, pamphlets, T-shirts, visual and audio materials to entertain, educate, and inspire you. We aim to distribute these through every available channel with every available technology—whether that means you are seeing anarchist classics at our bookfair stalls; reading our latest vegan cookbook at the café; downloading geeky fiction e-books; or digging new music and timely videos from our website.

PM Press is always on the lookout for talented and skilled volunteers, artists, activists, and writers to work with. If you have a great idea for a project or can contribute in some way, please get in touch.

PM Press
PO Box 23912
Oakland, CA 94623
510-658-3906 • info@pmpress.org

PM Press in Europe
europe@pmpress.org
www.pmpress.org.uk

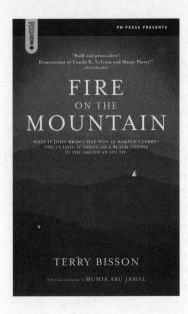

Fire on the Mountain

**Terry Bisson with an Introduction
by Mumia Abu-Jamal**
$15.95
ISBN: 978-1-60486-087-0
5 by 8 • 208 pages

It's 1959 in socialist Virginia. The Deep
South is an independent Black nation
called Nova Africa. The second Mars
expedition is about to touch down on
the red planet. And a pregnant scientist
is climbing the Blue Ridge in search of
her great-great grandfather, a teenage
slave who fought with John Brown
and Harriet Tubman's guerrilla army.

Long unavailable in the U.S., published in France as *Nova Africa*, *Fire on the
Mountain* is the story of what might have happened if John Brown's raid on
Harper's Ferry had succeeded—and the Civil War had been started not by
the slave owners but the abolitionists.

> *"History revisioned, turned inside out ... Bisson's
> wild and wonderful imagination has taken some
> strange turns to arrive at such a destination."*
> —Madison Smartt Bell, Anisfield-Wolf Award
> winner and author of Devil's Dream